Advertising For Love
Elisabeth Roseland

ADVERTISING FOR LOVE

First edition. May 18, 2017.

ISBN: 978-1941732069

Written by Elisabeth Roseland.

Dedication

To Christian, for being my Happily Ever After.

To Christa, for being my life raft and pulling me from the slush.

To Aunt Jeanne, for being my unwavering support. I miss you.

Chapter One

Tanya slid the black business card across the table. The gold script lettering glistened enticingly in the sun—*Ebony Nights*.

"You are out of your damn mind." Aisha crossed her arms and refused to touch it.

"Take it."

"No."

"Take it." Tanya tapped the card with her manicured nail.

"No." Aisha shook her head. "Didn't your mama teach you anything?"

Tanya sat back in her chair and laughed. "She sure did. She taught me to go after what I want and to always help a friend in need." She took a sip of her latte.

"Tanya." Aisha leaned across the table and lowered her voice. "I can't call them. It's illegal!"

"Technically, it's not illegal. They are simply a service that provides women with companionship for social events." She winked. "What you do after that event is over is up to you."

Aisha groaned. "How do you even know about them? I can't believe that you've actually used an..." she looked at the crowded tables around them and whispered, "...escort service."

Tanya smiled. "Renee hooked me up."

"Wait, Renee has called them?"

Tanya rolled her eyes. "Yes, girl. In fact, I think you're the only one who has not partaken of their services." She paused. "Except maybe Sherri. It would look bad for a deacon's wife to get a little paid action on the side." She smirked. "But then again, stranger things have happened."

Aisha picked her jaw off of the floor and sat back in her chair. "I can't—"

"Stop." Tanya held up her hand. "Let me break it down. First, you need someone—a male someone—to go with you to Hansen's black tie gala on Saturday. Because if you don't, you'll look like a loser with no social life, and you won't be able to keep that asshole Phil away from you, despite the fact that his wife will be there, probably throwing back martinis at the bar. Correct?"

"Hey!" Aisha objected. "Only half correct. Asshole Phil, yes. Most definitely, yes. But I'm not a loser."

"Whatever." Tanya took another sip of her drink. "You know I love you anyway. Second." She ticked the point off on her finger. "This place offers a smorgasbord of brothas." Aisha laughed. "Seriously. Whatever you're into, they've got it—dark, light, tall, short, muscular, slim." She paused, raising her eyebrows. "Big. Bigger."

"Tanya!"

"I'm serious. It's like shopping online. Choose your features and click 'buy it now'. Besides, when was the last time you got some?"

Aisha paused before answering. "It's been a while."

"'It's been a while'. Uh huh. That's what I thought. Not since that loser...uh...what was his name? You know, the one with the fucked-up car."

"Jamal."

"Jamal!" Tanya snapped her fingers. "That's right. He had the nerve to drive you around Chicago in that sputtering piece of shit. I'm surprised the hubcaps and mufflers and shit didn't start falling off of it when he got up to forty-five on the Drive. And really, I'm not one to be all up in your business, but if a man drives a car like that, can he really kick it into high gear between the sheets?"

"Okay, okay. You've got a point." She took a sip of her coffee. "And to answer your question. No. He didn't know how to handle business in the bedroom, which is just one of the reasons why we broke up."

"That and the fucked-up car."

"The fucked-up car, the fact that he was about to get fired from his job, his mama issues—too many problems to list. But this?" She gestured toward the card still sitting on the table. "I don't know if this is the answer."

"This is not a dating service, Aisha. This is an *escort* service." Tanya finished her latte. "You aren't buying a boyfriend. You're buying a bit of arm-candy for your company's event and a little after-hours action. Look." Tanya sat casually back in her chair. "I don't know why you would have a problem with this. You outsource half of your life anyway."

"What do you mean?"

"Oh, let's see..." Tanya paused when the El train rattled past them on the tracks overhead. As they waited for the din to subside, Aisha crossed her arms. Tanya simply smirked. The clatter quieted and she continued, "You hire someone to clean your house. You hire someone to plan your vacations. You take your clothes to the dry cleaners. Hell, you even get your groceries delivered."

"I hate grocery shopping," Aisha said defensively. "Besides, this is not the same thing. This is a person."

"This is a person providing a service, just like your cleaning lady. No difference."

"Huge difference. I'm not paying my cleaning lady to have sex with me."

"Well, maybe you should. It would probably be better than Jamal."

Aisha couldn't stop herself from laughing. "Have you seen my cleaning lady? She's like sixty-five and four feet tall."

"So? We're all the same height in the bed, and with the lights off, we can be as young as we want to be."

"Yeah, but can turning the lights off make you male?"

"Girl, anything in possible in the dark."

Aisha snickered. "You're crazy. You know that? There's medication for people with your condition."

"This right here"—she picked up the card—"is the only medicine I need." She put it back down on the table in front of her. "And you need to call them to cure what ails you."

Aisha still refused to touch it. "And what ails me?"

"Do you need a list? Let's see. Number one, you're a workaholic. Number two, you're commitment-phobic. Number three, you're a perfectionist. Number four—"

"Hold on, hold on. I'll give you the first one, sure. But the rest? No way. Commitment-phobic? Perfectionist? If those were true, then how do you explain Jamal?"

"Oh, that's easy." Tanya reached into her purse and pulled out her sunglasses to shield her eyes against the bright spring sun. "You knew from the get-go Jamal was wrong for you. That's why you went out with him. You didn't have to worry about getting emotionally involved with a guy who never stood a chance anyway. Plus, your relationships never last because any guy that makes it over to your place only has one thought."

"And what's that?"

"Damn. What does she need me for?"

Aisha stared at her. "What in the world does that mean?"

"Oh, you know what it means." Tanya dismissed her question with a wave of her hand. "Your place is hooked up. That view of the lake is fantastic. Plus, you drive a nice car and generally have your shit together. Most men take a look at all that and say, 'Damn, she's got all this? What am I bringing to this party?'"

Aisha raised one eyebrow. "So what you're saying is that men are intimidated by me?"

"Yep." Tanya punctuated her statement with a sharp nod of her head. "That's exactly what I am saying."

Before Aisha could protest, her cell phone rang. "Hold on, I have to take this. It's Sandra." She touched the Answer button. "Hello?"

"Sorry to bother you, Aisha. I know you're on your break but..." Sandra hesitated.

"That's okay. What is it?"

"Well..." Aisha could hear her nervousness. "Mr. Weinstein just called and he's still unhappy with the logo revisions. I tried to tell him he needed to talk to you about it, but he started yelling about how the design doesn't fit his image of the brand, and I told him I'm just the administrative assistant and I'd get in contact with you but he—"

"Don't worry about it. I'll take care of it when I get back."

"Okay." Sandra sounded relieved. "Thanks."

Aisha hung up the phone and turned her attention back toTanya, who raised her eyebrows. "Problems?"

"Nothing I can't take care of."

"You go 'head and handle your business. Told you that you were intimidating. Oh, speaking of which, when will you know if you got that promotion?"

Aisha sighed. "I don't know. A few weeks maybe. You know, I'll be pretty pissed if I don't get it, considering that last year I brought in the most revenue dollars—"

"And the economy was down."

Aisha nodded. "Right. And it would be *really* bad if they promoted Phil over me."

"Oooh, yeah. That would be bad. Like lawsuit bad."

Aisha shrugged. "I don't think it would get to that level, but—"

"But give a man some power over a beautiful woman, and watch him abuse it." Tanya pointed at her for emphasis. "Phil's already walking a fine line now with his behavior and how he looks at you. If he gets to be your boss, forget about it. You'll need to get a lawyer."

Aisha watched people jostle past each other on the busy street. On any given day in Chicago, the crowds were shoulder-to-shoulder but the first warm spring day of the season had turned the sidewalk into a traffic jam as everyone enjoyed the weather after months of oppressive winter.

Tanya's purse began ringing. She dug inside and pulled out her cell phone. "It's the office." She slid her finger across the phone's screen. "Hello?" She paused. "Okay, I'll be there in a minute. Tell him to hold on." She hung up. "I gotta go. The courier is there to pick up some papers I have to sign, and he's having a fit because they're not ready." She tapped the business card one more time before getting up. "Call them. They can't fix your intimidation problem, and they can't fix your Phil problem, but they can fix everything for Saturday night. Let them know I gave you their number. They're very exclusive and won't talk to you without a referral."

"Tanya, I don't know if—"

"Call them!" Tanya squeezed Aisha's shoulder before tossing her cup into the trash. "You won't regret it." She waved as she joined the steady stream of people on the sidewalk and scurried quickly down the street.

Aisha looked skeptically at the card for a moment before picking it up. She flipped it over; on the back was a phone number. No other information. She ran her finger thoughtfully over the edge of the card before slipping it into her purse.

Chapter Two

"Bill, it's Aisha. How are you doing today?" She adjusted her headset as she got comfortable in the desk chair.

"Aisha, I'm not happy with those logo revisions." Bill launched into the conversation without a greeting. "The spire is gone. We talked about the spire. It's been in the logo since my father started the company fifty years ago. It's a symbol of strength. People want to feel like they're dealing with a strong company and—"

"Bill, if I may stop you for a moment." Aisha could hear him breathing heavily on the other side of the phone. "You're right. However, the spire is also a symbol of a rigid hierarchy—of an institution—and in today's climate, Americans no longer trust their institutions and feel as though they've been betrayed by people in power. Companies like Enron, Lehman Brothers and Fannie Mae have all undermined Americans' faith in institutions, so while your father's logo may have worked in the past, it needs to be revamped to attract modern-day customers."

Bill paused. "Okay, I get that. But the circle? I don't know if the circle—"

"The shape of the circle evokes inclusiveness and unity. It gives people the sense that we're all in this together. Your company, sitting down next to the customer, helping to guide his or her financial decisions as opposed to sitting across a cold desk telling the customer what to do. Isn't that the image you want to portray to the general public?"

"Yes. Yes it is." Bill paused again. "Okay, I trust that you know what you're talking about, and I'll go along with it."

"Great. You won't be disappointed. Oh, and one more thing." She had been waiting for the right moment to make her pitch. "I really think you need to add at least one TV commercial to your package."

"I don't have the—"

Aisha didn't give him the chance to object. "I know you said you're working with a limited budget, but a thirty-second spot shown during the six o'clock local newscast will hit millions of your target consumers. Combine that TV spot with the radio spots we already have planned, and the number of people you reach will increase exponentially."

"Aisha, it's just not in our budget."

"Okay, just think about it." She pulled up her email and attached a file before pressing send. "I'm sending you some numbers to look over." She then readjusted her headset to make sure Bill heard the next thing she said. "And I do want you to know I have it on good authority that Welden and Sons out of Indiana is making a move into the larger market over the next couple of months, and their ad campaign includes radio spots, two thirty-second TV commercials to run concurrently and several billboards." She paused. "I thought you might want to know."

Bill fell silent. "Okay. Thanks for that information. I'll look over those numbers and get back to you."

"You're welcome. It was a pleasure speaking to you. As always." She hung up the phone and removed her headset. She then printed out a copy of the email she sent him and stood up to file it in her filing cabinet.

"Knock knock."

Aisha turned from her paperwork and groaned silently to herself. "Hey, Phil. What's up?"

Phil stood in the doorway of her office. As usual, beads of sweat dotted his forehead. His watery blue eyes bounced up and down Aisha's body, lingering a bit too long on her breasts.

"Hi, Aisha." He leaned against the doorframe in an attempt to look casual. "I was wondering if you were going to the gala on Saturday night."

She nodded sharply and then sat down at her desk. At least she could hide her long legs from his hungry stare. "I am. Are you?"

"Yes, I'm going." He grinned. Aisha grimaced at his crooked, coffee-stained teeth.

"That's nice. I'm looking forward to seeing Karen again."

"Oh, she can't go." Phil put his hands in his pockets and moved them up and down, jiggling his change. At least, Aisha hoped that was all he was jiggling. "She's taking the kids to Wisconsin to see her mother for the weekend." He paused and then smiled again. "So I'll be there by myself. What about you? Are you going alone?"

Aisha watched as a bead of sweat coursed down the side of his face. His eager eyes awaited her answer. "Um...no." She faced her computer. "I'm bringing someone."

"Oh, that's too bad. I was hoping I'd have someone to stand in the corner with. Maybe have a dance partner."

She kept her eyes glued to the screen. "No, sorry. My dance card is full."

"Oh, okay." She could hear him breathing as he continued to stare at her. She shot him a sideways glance and then went back to her computer. "I'll...uh...see you later then." He walked out.

"See ya, Phil."

She slumped back in her chair and stared out her window. From thirty-five stories up, she had a breathtaking view of downtown. The sun reflected off the majestic skyscrapers—an eclectic mix of early twentieth century stone and concrete and modern-day glass and steel. It had taken her many years of hard work and absolute commitment to her job to attain that view, the office and the position that came with it. Thanks in no small part to her, Hansen Advertising secured several new clients in the past year. She had gotten accolades from her boss, a large bonus and a feeling of job security, but... She sighed as her eyes darted about her impersonal office. *Workaholic? Commitment-phobic? Perfectionist?* Unlike most of her colleagues, there were no family pictures, no kids' scribbling masterpieces and no cute Mother's Day cards. There were some Certificates of Appreciation on the wall, her

Employee of the Year award on the bookshelf and a paperweight her nephew had made for her on the desk.

Aisha reached down in her purse and pulled out the sleek, black card. *Ebony Nights.* The words tempted her. She got up from her desk and closed her office door. On the back of the card, the 312 number dipped and curved elegantly. Somewhere in the Loop, perhaps within walking distance of Aisha's office, men were waiting to be chosen. *What did Tanya say? Pick your features? Just "buy it now"?* Aisha laughed quietly at the memory. *Besides, I only need a date to the gala. I'm not ordering a prostitute. I'm getting some Phil repellent. I'm not buying sex from a stranger. That would be too weird.*

She picked up her cell phone and dialed the number before she could change her mind.

"Hello?"

"Um...hello. Is this *Ebony Nights*?"

"Yes, it is." The woman's crisp and professional voice immediately impressed Aisha. "Who referred you?"

Tanya's comment about exclusivity came to mind. "Tanya," she replied. "Tanya Roberts."

"One moment, please." Aisha could hear typing. After a few moments, the woman seemed to find the needed information. "Yes. How can we help you?"

"I...uh..." Aisha struggled to find a way to ask for what she was looking for. "I have an event I need to go to and...I...um..."

"When is the event?"

Aisha exhaled, grateful to be answering an easy question. "Saturday night."

"Formal or casual?"

"Formal."

"Business related or personal event?"

"Business." Aisha could hear typing as she answered the woman's questions.

"Thank you." More clicking. "Now. I'm going to ask you a series of personal attributes questions."

"Okay."

"Age. Twenties? Thirties? Forties? Fifties? Sixties?"

Sixties? There are sixty-year-olds working as escorts? Aisha shuddered at the thought. "Thirties."

"Preferred height. Five-nine to six feet? Six-one to six-three? Six-four or taller?

"Um...Six feet to six-three." Aisha began to get excited. At five-eight herself, she could wear her killer heels and still be with someone taller. That was most definitely not the case with short Jamal—yet another one of his issues.

"Skin color—light, medium, dark or no preference?"

"No preference." All of them sounded perfectly fine to her.

"Hair—bald, short, long, dreads."

"Um, either bald or short. No dreads." Aisha immediately thought back to her high school boyfriend. His dreads were one of the things that had attracted her to him. Then again, it had been the nineties.

"Languages—English only, English and Spanish, or English and French?"

Wow, this is getting specific. "English only is fine."

The click of the keys echoed in Aisha's ear as the woman typed. "All right. I have input your preferences. A few notes about our policies. Our rates are two hundred dollars an hour or five hundred dollars for five hours. Please note the contract entitles you to the company and conversation of one gentleman for the agreed upon time. *Ebony Nights* does not condone or encourage anything that goes beyond the boundaries of the contract. Is this understood?"

Aisha blinked at the legal disclaimer. "Yes."

"Good." More typing. "We guarantee the gentleman will be on time, courteous, respectful and discreet. If, for some reason, you are dissatisfied with your experience, we offer a 100% money back guarantee. We take Visa, Master Card and American Express. Which one will you be using?"

A 100% money back guarantee? Very professional. Perhaps Tanya was right. Dry cleaners, grocery delivery, cleaning lady and now, professional escort—*add another item to the list of things that can be outsourced.* "I'll be using American Express." She opened her wallet and eagerly gave her information to the woman over the phone.

Chapter Three

Saturday night, Aisha stood in her bedroom surveying her clothing options. A short red dress, a low-cut black gown and a black, sleeveless sheath lay strewn on the bed. One highlighted her legs, one brought attention to her breasts and the other was the conservative option. She thought about Phil's roving eyes and the possibility that the escort might be a psycho and made an easy decision. "Conservative," she muttered. "Definitely conservative."

As she dressed and put on her makeup, she plotted out her evening. Greet him with a handshake, introduce him as a "friend", stick to talking about the weather and the crappy economy and by all means, keep it professional. Aisha applied her dark red lipstick and softly rubbed her lips together. *What kind of man becomes an escort anyway? Is he even attractive? Can he put two sentences together? Is he addicted to drugs?* Aisha stopped brushing her hair. "Damn it," she whispered. In her desire to quickly purchase Phil repellent, she hadn't even thought of that possibility. "If he shows up high," she said to the empty room, "I'll 'escort' his ass right out of there." *Thank God for the 100% money back guarantee.*

She swept her hair up into a twist and secured it with bobby pins. For the formal event, she had experimented with her makeup and chosen smoky eye shadow and dramatic blush that complimented her dark brown eyes and caramel skin. She stepped into her sheath dress, zipped it up and slipped on her three-inch heels. Aisha took a step back and admired herself in the floor-length mirror. "You look good." She put her hands on her hips. "Even if you do have to resort to buying your dates."

She gripped the steering wheel as she whizzed down Lake Shore Drive. *What if he gets drunk and embarrasses me? What if he makes inappropriate comments?* She chuckled. If that happened, no one would bat an eye. Getting drunk and being inappropriate was par for the course at every Hansen social function. She thought back to last year's event. Her boss and some of the other vice presidents had started a conga line on the dance floor. One of the women had stepped on the dress of the woman in front of her, and half of the line had crashed to the floor. Fortunately, Aisha had refused to be part of the spectacle and stood in the corner nursing her pinot grigio while trying to pretend to enjoy Andre's company. She leaned back in her seat as she eased up on the accelerator. Andre was another dating mistake—insecure because he never finished college and because she made more money than he did.

As she approached downtown, Aisha could see the moonlight reflecting off of the dark, churning waters of Lake Michigan. The soaring skyscrapers were outlined by thousands of lights from quiet offices and late night workers; their illuminated antennae flashed red warnings into the night.

Greg. That's all she knew about him. His name was Greg, and he fit her specifications—six foot to six-three, in his thirties, bald or short hair. Not much information to go on, but it filled her order. She shook her head. *How did I let Tanya convince me to order a person?*

She weaved her way through the downtown streets before arriving at the hotel. Hansen spared no expense when it came to their galas, and they were always held in a ballroom of one of the most elegant hotels in the city. The driveway sparkled under the light of hundreds of bulbs. As Aisha pulled up, one of the valets ran out to open her door.

"Are you going to the Hansen gala, ma'am?"

"Um, yes." Aisha's stomach suddenly flipped over. She swallowed hard. "I am."

The valet held out his hand to help her out of the car. Hers trembled as she reached for it, almost slipping out of his grip. *Get a hold of yourself. You don't actually have to talk to him. Just sit there and eat, drink your wine, listen to the presentation and watch people get stupid on the dance floor. Talking is not necessary. Not talking to him is better than being alone and fighting off an increasingly drunk Phil all night.* She took a deep breath, stepped out of the car with renewed confidence and walked into the hotel.

Her eyes scanned the bustling lobby. Some of her coworkers breezed by dressed in silk, satin and sequins. She tried to look casual and nodded and waved as they headed toward the ballroom, however her eyes constantly scanned the room for six feet to six-three, in his thirties, bald or short hair.

"You must be Aisha." A deep baritone voice surprised her from behind. She turned and came face-to-face with sparkling eyes and a perfect smile.

"Greg?" Aisha's butterflies immediately disappeared. His skin was rich and brown, the color of milk chocolate, and his hair was close cut and neat. He towered over her despite the fact that she wore her three-inch heels, and she took quiet pleasure in having to tilt her head up to look at him. Dressed in a formal tux, Greg looked like he belonged at the party and would fit right in.

"It's a pleasure to meet you." He leaned in and gave her a soft, gentle hug. Aisha caught a whiff of his cologne—fresh and clean. As he lightly squeezed her, she wrapped her arms around his broad back. The formal clothes were hiding a powerful, solid frame. She sighed. *Perfect.*

"It's a pleasure to meet you as well."

"Nervous?" A slight grin crossed his face.

"Not anymore."

"Ah, you were worried I'd be an inappropriate hot mess who would completely embarrass you at your company's function." His brown eyes twinkled mischievously.

The room suddenly felt warm as she shyly glanced down at the floor. "Okay, I have to admit I had some concerns." She looked back up at him. He stared at her intensely with a hint of a smile on his face. "I'm glad to see, however, my fears were unfounded."

"Well, I'm pleased I've met with your expectations." He took her hand and wrapped it comfortably around his forearm. "Shall we go in?"

With the gentlemanly move, Aisha's butterflies returned. "Okay." And the two of them entered the ballroom.

The music from the live band filled the room and mingled with the laughs and loud conversations of already tipsy partygoers. Aisha went to the main table and checked in.

"Aisha! So glad you could make it," Jennifer squealed from across the table. Despite the emotion in her voice, Jennifer's face barely moved. She must have spent the day in her plastic surgeon's office getting a few touch-up injections. "And who's your handsome date?"

"Oh, this is Greg. Greg, this is Jennifer."

Greg extended his hand. "Pleasure to meet you, Jennifer."

She clasped his hand with both of hers. "Oh, no, the pleasure's all mine." Jennifer's eyes remained glued on Greg. "No fair, Aisha. You've been holding out on us."

"Ha. Funny." Aisha quickly glanced around and spotted the nearest vacant corner. "Okay, we'll talk to you later." With a wave of her hand, she headed out of the crowd and retreated to a quieter spot.

Greg followed her to the corner of the room and stared at her for a moment before speaking. "You don't particularly enjoy these things, do you?"

Aisha rolled her eyes. "Is it that obvious?"

Greg smirked. "Yes. Yes it is." He stepped in front of her, blocking her view of the overcrowded dance floor. "Then why go? Why not spend the night at home or go out with your girls instead?"

"Because." Aisha glanced around Greg. She caught a glimpse of her boss dancing a bit too closely with the head of IT. "I have to be here. To show my face. To be a team player. I'm up for a promotion, and well...it's better if I attend these things."

Greg nodded. "Shall we get a drink?"

"Yes, please." He took her arm again and graciously led her through the crowd to the bar.

"What would you like?"

"A glass of pinot grigio."

Greg turned to the bartender. "One pinot grigio and one glass of soda water please." The bartender poured their drinks. Greg handed Aisha her wine. "Salud." He lifted his glass and touched hers.

"Salud." She smiled and took a sip. Greg did the same. "So." Aisha pointed at his glass. "You don't drink?"

He smiled. "Not while I'm working."

Aisha laughed quietly and lifted the glass to her lips, enjoying the dry, smooth taste as it slid over her tongue. "Hey, you know, I just realized I don't even know your last name. What is it?"

"It's Williams. And yours?"

"Anderson."

"Anderson." He paused. "Aisha Anderson."

She held up her hand. "Yeah, yeah, I know. AA. I've heard all the jokes. Hey, AA, you working the twelve steps?"

Greg laughed. "Actually, I was going to say that I like your name." He took a step closer to her. "Aisha Anderson. It's very alliterative."

Aisha's heart beat furiously in her chest. Their eyes met. She averted her gaze back to the dance floor. "Thanks," she mumbled and took another sip. The lead singer of the band made the dinner announcement, much to her relief, and she and Greg pushed their way through the crowd to find their assigned table.

"Carl. Mandy. Good to see you," Aisha greeted her coworkers at the table as she sat down.

"Hey, Aisha." Mandy leaned in and gave her a quick hug. "I'm so glad you're sitting next to me. We have to catch up. It's been forever. You remember my husband, Doug? I can't believe the numbers I've been seeing from your team. Unbelievable. I know Phil must be shitting in envy." She tilted her head back and gulped down the last few drops of her red wine. "Hey, who's your date?"

"This is Greg. Greg, this is Mandy. She works in accounting."

Greg leaned across Aisha and extended his hand. "Pleasure to meet you, Mandy."

"Greg." Mandy shook his hand. When he sat back in his chair, she whispered to Aisha, "He's gorgeous. Who is he? Where did you meet him? Why haven't I met him before?"

"Well..."

"Excuse me, ladies." The waiter placed their salads in front of them. Aisha exhaled. She hadn't come up with a cover story. "Shall I refill your glasses?"

"I thought you'd never ask." Mandy winked at the waiter. "Red, please." The burgundy liquid swirled around the glass.

"White for me, thanks." The waiter poured Aisha's wine and gave the bottle a twist when he finished. "So how are things down in accounting?"

Mandy picked up her fork. "Oh, you know. Same old, same old. We had to cut two admin assistants, and everyone's biting their nails over who's next." She took a bite of her salad. "So I hear you applied for Vicki's job."

"I did." She lifted a wilted piece of lettuce drenched in dressing and skeptically took a bite. "What else have you heard?"

"Well,"—Mandy glanced at her—"you did hear the rumor about why she quit, right?"

"Yeah, something about not feeling like the other vice presidents took her ideas seriously. So she got an opportunity at another company where she thought she could really contribute. We only had a brief conversation in the hallway about it."

"Well, it was a little more than that." Mandy took another sip of her wine. "You know Eva and Vicki are friends, and Eva told me Vicki said that when all the vice presidents get together it's awful—dirty jokes, sexual innuendo, that kind of stuff. Not directed at her. Not anything too blatant, but enough to make her feel very uncomfortable."

"Really?"

"Yeah. You know she's the only woman VP. Or, at least she was."

Aisha exhaled sharply. "Yes, but I had no idea that kind of stuff was going on."

"But I'm sure you'll be fine," Mandy said with a wave of her hand. "You're no push-over. I've seen how you handle the toughest clients. It's damn impressive. Plus, your only competition is Phil, and no one can stand that perv. Have you seen him tonight?"

"Thankfully, no."

"Stay away. He's hitting on every woman in the place and generally embarrassing himself and being an ass." She took another sip. "As usual." Aisha chuckled. "So..." Mandy leaned across Aisha, almost ending up in her lap. "What do you do, Greg?"

Aisha almost choked on a tomato. "He...uh ..."

"Well, I used to be an investment banker," Greg answered calmly. "But you can imagine how far that career took me." Mandy laughed. "So after I left that field, I decided to go to culinary school."

"Oooh, so you're a chef?"

"Yes, although currently a chef with no restaurant. I'm in the process of opening my own."

"Aisha!" Mandy nudged her playfully. "You didn't tell me your boyfriend is a chef."

"Uh...he's not my—"

"Excuse me, ma'am." The waiter reached from behind her, took her uneaten salad and placed in front of her a chicken breast swimming in sauce. Two dried-out potato wedges and a spring of something that may or may not have been rosemary sat on the corner of the plate.

"Wow. Looks delicious, huh?" Mandy said sarcastically. Aisha attempted to cut into the chicken. She struggled to get the knife through. Mandy held up a withered potato on the end of her fork. "I know most of the money from the tickets went to the homeless shelter, but you'd think that dinner could have been halfway decent."

"Classic catering mistake." Greg took a small bite of the chicken. "Chicken is tricky. It has to be well done, or else you risk some serious gastro-intestinal distress. And when serving chicken to a group as large as this one, you really have to be careful because mishandling food could lead to ruining your reputation at best and a lawsuit at worst So some caterers think the only way to ensure food safety is to cook the hell out of it. Although,"—he scooped up a bit of the sauce with a spoon and tasted it—"the sauce isn't bad. But I would've used a chardonnay instead of a moscato. It's less sweet." He tasted it again. "It could also use more lemon and salt."

Aisha stared at him, unable to speak. He flashed his perfect smile at her and winked. At a loss for words, she simply shook her head and took another sip from her glass. She then remembered Tanya's insinuation that a little after-hours action could also be purchased, and despite her earlier reservation, Aisha began to consider the possibility.

"Aisha," Mandy said a bit too loudly, her most recent glass of wine apparently kicking in. "Where did you find this guy?"

Aisha took another drink, furiously trying to come with something. "I...uh..."

"Oh, we go way back." Greg slipped his hand underneath the table and gave her knee a firm squeeze. "We're old family friends."

Aisha felt the warmth from his hand resting on her lap. She had the urge to take it and guide it upward to between her legs. The wetness grew between her thighs as she looked at him. His brown eyes, full lips, perfect smile, smooth skin—everything about him radiated intelligent, sexy confidence. Greg read the expression on her face. He raised one eyebrow slightly and slowly moved his hand up her leg.

"Well, thank God for family," Mandy yelled. "Speaking of, you wouldn't happen to have any brothers, would you?"

Greg continued to stare knowingly at Aisha before turning his attention to Mandy. He also removed his hand, much to her dismay. "No, I'm sorry. I don't."

Mandy banged her hand on the table, causing all of the plates to rattle. "Isn't that always the way? I've got a single sister, but the good ones are always taken." Aisha glanced over at Doug, who disappeared more and more into his chair as his wife's volume increased. He also signaled the waiter to bring him another beer.

"How is Alison, by the way?" Aisha attempted to redirect the conversation.

"A mess. You know she lost her job, right? So she had to move back in with my parents out in Palos. Oh, and her car got repoed. And the day they came to get it she had been in an accident and..." Mandy continued her rambling tale, but Aisha wasn't really listening. She couldn't stop focusing on Greg's touch. Where he had placed his hand pulsated with energy. She wanted his hands to touch her in other places. His mouth too.

A bland and unfulfilling dessert concluded the meal, and when the presentation part of the evening began, Aisha gratefully turned her attention to the CEO. He presented slides outlining the company's achievements over the last year, which included donating hundreds of thousands of dollars to charitable organizations, launching a green initiative and securing several new, lucrative clients.

"...and she doesn't know I'm about to do this, but I would like to acknowledge the woman who helped to ensure Hansen Advertising stays ahead of the competition—Aisha Anderson."

Aisha's hand froze while in the process of bringing her glass to her lips. Her face flushed as everyone clapped for her.

"Stand up, Aisha."

She set her glass back down on the table and reluctantly stood, quickly acknowledged everyone with a slight wave of her hand, and then sat down. The room felt twenty degrees warmer.

"Congratulations," Greg whispered in her ear. He then put his hand on her shoulder, squeezed it gently and slowly rubbed her back. Aisha leaned into him.

"Thank you. I had no idea he was going to do that. I'm so embarrassed."

"You handled it well." His face mere inches from hers, Aisha had the urge to kiss him, to feel his soft lips and his warm, wet tongue. She held his gaze for a moment before forcing herself to turn her attention back to the CEO. Greg put his hand back on her shoulder and pulled her into him. With his leg pressed firmly against hers, she found it impossible to concentrate on the remainder of the presentation.

Once the CEO finished speaking, the band retook the stage. Mandy gave Aisha an awkward, off-balance hug and tripped her way to the dance floor, pulling a reluctant Doug behind her.

"So." Greg's eyes twinkled. "Single-handedly responsible for the success of Hansen Advertising."

With his arm on the back of her chair, he slowly stroked Aisha's bare shoulder. It gave her goose bumps. "Well, maybe not 'single-handedly', but perhaps double or triple-handedly."

Greg chuckled softly. The deep, sensual sound made her want to rip his fine tux right off him. She forced her hands to remain in her lap. "Hmm. Smart, successful, beautiful and funny." He brought a hand up to the side of her face and stroked it. He leaned into her.

"Hey, Aisha." Phil's voice tore her gaze away from Greg's approaching lips.

She sighed. "Hello, Phil."

Phil glanced at Greg before turning his attention back to her. "Congrats on all your good work this year."

"Thanks." She flashed what she hoped passed for a genuine smile. "But you know, we all made our contribution."

"Hmm." Phil nodded slightly in response and then again looked at Greg.

After a moment, Aisha said, "Oh, this is Greg." Greg got up from his chair. Aisha did the same. "Greg, this is Phil."

"Nice to meet you, Phil." Greg was several inches taller, and Phil shrank back as Greg shook his hand.

"Uh, yeah, nice to meet you too." He shifted from one foot to the other and then took another sip from his beer. As he did so, he stared at Aisha's breasts from over the rim of his glass. "Um, Aisha, I hope you don't mind me saying so, but you look beautiful tonight."

Aisha's eyes narrowed as she watched Phil's dirty mind devour her body. Before she had the chance to say anything, Greg slipped his arm around her waist and hugged her close. "I was just telling her the same thing."

Phil's gaze left Aisha's body and snapped up to meet Greg's glare. Greg said nothing and simply stared at him in quiet confrontation. Phil swallowed hard. "Um, yeah, well, congrats again. I'll see you later." He then scurried off.

"Bye," she called after him and then turned to Greg. "You're terrible, you know that?"

"What?" He raised his eyebrows. "What did I do?"

"Sent him off running with his tail between his legs."

Greg put his other hand around her waist and pressed himself against her. Aisha could feel the hard contours of his body, and her pussy tingled with pleasure. "I don't like that guy." He stared off in the direction of Phil's exit before gazing back down at her. "Be careful around him." He frowned. "Better yet, stay away from him."

Aisha placed one hand on his firm chest. She wanted to slowly undo all of the buttons on his starched shirt and stroke his bare muscles with her fingers as she kissed him. Instead, she patted him gently. "Oh, don't you worry." She tilted her head up to him. "I avoid Phil like the plague."

"You better. Hey, would you like to dance?"

"I would love to."

Greg slipped his hand into hers and led her to the dance floor.

As they danced, Aisha could not stop wondering how his moves would translate to more horizontal activities. His rhythm and timing during the fast songs were perfectly coordinated, and when the band began to play a slow number, he pulled her into him. Aisha gasped when he wrapped his arms around her and swayed in tune with the music.

"So did you have a good time tonight?" He whispered in her ear.

"I did, yes." She smiled up at him. "Thank you."

"The pleasure was all mine. I had a great time as well." He took her hand in his and brought it up to his chest, and shivers of desire ran up and down her spine.

"Well, I think I've had enough corporate socializing for one night." Aisha glanced over Greg's shoulder to see the entire human resources department huddled in a circle, swaying off-beat to the music. Someone slipped and three people almost fell to the floor. Aisha looked back up at Greg. "Yes, most definitely enough corporate socializing for one night."

"Understandable." Greg's other hand trailed its way down to the small of her back. She wanted him to move it lower, pull up the hem of her dress and slip his fingers inside her. She bit her lip softly at the thought of it and quickly turned away. "So tell me." Greg bent down so his lips were almost touching her ear. "What would you like to do now?" His warm breath caressed her neck.

"Well." Aisha paused, just for a moment. "We could go to my place, if that's okay with you."

The look on his face made her hungry for him. "That's fine with me."

Chapter Four

They both got into their cars, and Greg followed Aisha back to her condo. During the short ride back, she thought about what she was going to do. It didn't feel like prostitution, but she had to admit to herself that it was. Places on her body still throbbed with energy from Greg's touch—the small of her back, her bare arm, her thigh. She had to have more. Whatever his price, she'd pay it to have that mouth kissing hers, to feel those hands touching her skin, to have his hard naked body pressed up against hers. She squirmed in her seat at the mere thought of it.

"So this is it." Aisha opened the front door.

"Very nice." Greg looked around. "Beautiful view." He walked toward the balcony overlooking the lake.

"Thanks." Aisha closed the front door and set her keys and purse down on the table. When she turned around, Greg grabbed her and pulled her to him.

"You are absolutely beautiful." He touched the side of her face, leaned down and kissed her.

His tongue parted her lips. Aisha returned his warm, wet kisses and wrapped her arms around him.

"Mmm." Greg broke the kiss and looked deep into her eyes. "I've been wanting to do that since I first saw you in the lobby."

Aisha giggled, slightly embarrassed. "So have I." Suddenly shy, Aisha couldn't bring herself to look at him. "So what do we do now?"

"Whatever you'd like," he whispered.

Heat radiated from his body. "I...uh...don't know how you normally handle these things." She cleared her throat. "Do I... I mean how much extra..." She couldn't bring herself to finish the question. In fact, she didn't know what question to ask.

"Let's do this." Greg put one hand on the side of her face. "Let's see how things go and then talk money afterwards." His deep brown eyes scanned her face. "Is that okay?"

"Yes. That's okay."

"Good." He put his other hand on her hip and grabbed her firmly. Even through his suit, Aisha could feel his solid and powerful body. She wanted it on top of her. He bent down and slowly kissed her again, his lips teasing hers. As his kisses grew hungrier, Aisha grew wet with excitement.

She could feel him stiffening, his erection rubbing enticingly against her thigh. He continued to kiss her as he removed his jacket, allowing it to fall to the floor in a soft heap. He wrapped his arms around her and gave her ass a firm squeeze. She allowed her hands to wander down to the front of his pants and massaged his cock. He grunted at her touch, and slid his hands up to unzip the back of her dress. As it slipped off, Greg directed his skillful kisses to her neck and with one hand stroked her breasts through her black lace bra.

He then pulled back. "Shall we take this to the bedroom?"

Aisha smiled and led him down the hall. As she walked in front of him, she was hyper aware of the fact that she only wore her underwear and heels. Normally, she wouldn't have felt comfortable in such an obviously sexy get-up, but the way Greg looked at her as they headed for the bedroom made her feel completely at ease. His gaze consumed her body as they danced over her full breasts, round hips and long legs.

"Mmm, Aisha. You are sexy." Aisha squealed as he pulled her into him, rubbing himself slowly against her ass. His cock was like a rock through his pants, and she was eager for him to take everything off so she could see if it looked as good as it felt.

Once in the bedroom, she faced him. He kissed her softly again, and she slowly began to undress him. Aisha loosened his tie and unbuttoned his shirt, smiling with pleasure at his muscular arms. She pulled up his sleeveless, white undershirt and let her fingers dance over his skin. Every inch of his torso had been chiseled in stone. She ran her hands over the hard contours and Greg's breath quickened.

He grabbed her and kissed her again. With one hand, he unsnapped her bra. Aisha shuddered as he squeezed her breasts and rubbed his thumb over her nipples until they responded. She took off her underwear, tossing it to the side with a small kick. She then slipped off her heels, and with both hands eagerly undid his belt and loosened his pants. As they fell to the floor, she slipped her hands between his boxers and his powerful thighs and pushed them down as well.

The sight of his large cock standing at attention made her mouth water. She wrapped her hand around it and stroked it softly. Greg groaned, led her to the bed and lay her down. Once horizontal, he planted a kiss on her neck, licking the soft skin right above her collarbone. Aisha closed her eyes and ran her hands down Greg's broad back.

"Now. I just have one. Question. To ask. You." Greg punctuated each word with a kiss as he made his way down her body. He stopped at her breasts, took her left nipple into his mouth, and sucked and pulled gently. The gentle pressure of his teeth and the roughness of his tongue made Aisha writhe beneath him.

"What's that?" she croaked.

"How many orgasms do you want to have?" Greg took her right nipple into his mouth and sucked and pulled again. Aisha's breath caught in her throat, rendering her speechless. "And I have to tell you there's a two orgasm minimum."

"What did you say?"

Greg slid up to face her and his body rubbed against hers. She wrapped her right leg around him, enjoying the feel of his soft skin, the taught muscles flexing and contracting underneath the surface.

"I said." A smile played at the corner of his mouth. "How many orgasms do you want to have? You must have at least two. Those are the rules."

"Really? And whose rules are these?"

"Mine." The grin made its full appearance. "But it's at least two. If you'd like to have more, I'd be happy to oblige."

Aisha laughed. "You've got to be kidding me. Two orgasms? You mean tonight? As in before you leave?"

"Yes, of course. Don't tell me you've never had two in one evening before."

She snorted. "I don't always have one, let alone two."

"Well." Greg placed his finger directly on her clit and pressed down gently. Aisha gasped. "We're going to have to change that."

"Okay, two it is then." She pushed the back of her head deep into the pillow and lifted her hips in response to Greg's touch. He removed his hand, and Aisha bit her lip in anticipation as he slowly worked his way down her body with his tongue. The wetness traced its way down to her belly button. He tickled it with his mouth and she giggled. She looked down to see Greg grinning up at her as he approached her pussy. The mere thought of his tongue caressing her clit was almost too much, and she wanted to tell Greg to hurry up and lick her. But he took his time, rubbing his face into her dark, course hairs and kissing the insides of her thighs. His breath caressed her sensitive skin, and inside her body screamed that it wanted him now, but Greg took his slow, delicious time.

Finally, he parted her lips with his fingers and ran his tongue up her juicy folds. Aisha arched her back and moaned. Greg explored the opening to her pussy, rimming it before pushing his tongue inside her. She shuddered. Glancing down, she could only see the top of Greg's head, so she closed her eyes and concentrated on the sensations. He wriggled his tongue inside her with an undulating rhythm that made Aisha grip the sheets. Slowly at first, before increasing his delicious tempo to a speed that made Aisha's breath falter. With his hands, he pushed on the insides of her thighs, and she became aware that she was practically crushing Greg's head between them.

Her eyes flew open. "Sorry," she wheezed, finding it difficult to speak.

"Hey, no problem." Greg lifted his head. "That just means I'm doing a good job." He bent down again and gave her pussy a quick lick from bottom to top, stopping briefly at her clit to tickle it with the tip of his tongue.

Aisha let out a sound halfway between a grunt and a yell, and her hips jerked upward. Greg slipped his hands underneath her and gripped her ass, repositioning her pussy close to his face. This time, he licked her with the full surface of his tongue, and Aisha could feel its roughness caressing every inch of her. He moved from south to north again, over and over, each time stimulating her from the opening of her pussy to her clit. Aisha felt herself grow wetter and wetter with each pass of his tongue, and the sound of Greg devouring her filled her ears and sent shivers down her spine.

"Don't st—" was all she could get out before she came, arching her back so violently that Greg had to grab her ass even more firmly to hold her in place. Her orgasm rushed through her like a current, setting every pore ablaze. Greg kept stroking her with his tongue as she came, and the sensation soon became too much as her senses went into overload. "Enough." She grunted. "That's enough."

Greg let her go, and as he sat up, she could still feel the imprint of his hands on her ass from where he struggled to restrain her. She kept her eyes closed as the residual shockwaves rippled through her body. Every inch of her felt alive.

"Good?" Greg's voice whispered in her ear.

Unable to speak, Aisha simply nodded.

"Good. That's just number one."

Number one lit her whole body on fire. Number one hit her like a brick wall. Number one was enough. "No." She forced herself to speak. "No more. One is enough."

"Oh, no." Aisha still had her eyes closed, but she could hear the glee in his voice. "I've got a reputation to uphold. Two orgasm minimum, remember?"

"No." Aisha still couldn't open her eyes, but at least she could talk a little better. "I'm good."

Greg chuckled softly. "We'll see about that." She heard him get up from the bed. She forced her eyes open to see him rummaging around in his discarded pants pocket.

"What are you looking for?"

"This." He held up the condom in his hand.

"I don't think..." Aisha let the shaking of her head finish her sentence.

A spark lit up in Greg's eyes. "Oh, I think you can." In an instant, he was on top of her again, kissing her neck and rubbing his thumbs over her nipples.

Her body jolted, and an unexpected moan escaped from her lips. She grew wet again as his hard cock rubbed against her leg, and she couldn't stop the words from tumbling out of her mouth. "Inside me, now."

Greg slipped on the condom, grabbed her left leg, hitched it up around his back and entered her. Aisha arched her back as his cock slid inside. "Damn woman, mmm."

His rhythm was slow and sensual, just like his dance moves. He interlocked his fingers with hers, pushed her hands above her head and ran his tongue slowly down her neck. Aisha cocked her legs back, allowing him to penetrate her deeper, and they both groaned with pleasure. He bent down to kiss her, and Aisha could taste herself on his lips. His talented tongue explored her mouth, and Aisha relished the opportunity to devour him—his soft mouth, his full lips, his hungry kisses. She let go of his hands and wrapped her arms around his back, digging her fingers into his tight skin and pulling him close.

"Faster," Aisha whispered, and Greg's hands made their way down to her hips and held them firmly. With strength and power, he rammed himself into her. Aisha held on tighter as she took in his entire cock, groaning with each of Greg's thrusts. The intensity and speed increased, rocking the bed back and forth and making the headboard bang noisily against the wall. Orgasm number two caught her by surprise. It started between her legs and then radiated up and down her body. Powerless to stop her convulsions, she could only sigh as the waves of pleasure overtook her. As they began to subside, Greg's body shook with his own orgasm. He grunted for a few moments, his firm, brown chest only inches from hers. With one hand, she stroked it as he came, until he finally rolled off of her, collapsing onto the bed.

Aisha couldn't speak. She struggled to catch her breath, and sweat dripped off her body. Every pore tingled. She could hear Greg's belabored breathing slow down next to her.

"I told you that you had number two in you," he said with a voice hoarse from exertion.

Aisha stared at the ceiling. "I didn't believe it was possible."

Greg inhaled deeply and then exhaled, now in control. "What I can't believe is that a beautiful woman like you sometimes has sex with a man and doesn't come at all. I hear that all the time. How can you let men be so selfish?"

Aisha shrugged and glanced over at him. "I don't know. Sometimes you don't really feel like it. Sometimes you're in a hurry, and he won't quit bugging you so you just give him some so he'll be happy. Sometimes he doesn't really know what he's doing, so you just encourage him to finish so you can do something else."

"Do something else?" Greg raised his eyebrows. "Like what?"

"Like watch TV. Or get something to eat. Or go to sleep."

Greg laughed heartily. "Really? Watching TV is better than having sex?"

"Sometimes, yes. It depends what's on." The echoes of their laughter filled the room before they both fell silent. Aisha took a deep breath, contentment washing over her. She then glanced at the glowing clock on her nightstand. Her five hours were almost over.

"Okay, so there really is no way to tactfully say this, so I'm just going to ask. How much?"

Greg simply looked at her. He said nothing. For a moment, Aisha wondered if she'd offended him in some way. The expression on his face, however, was not one of anger. In fact, he seemed a little nervous.

He finally spoke. "Um, actually." He paused and looked away. "Um, please don't think this is a line or anything, but I would really rather have your phone number instead. I'd like to take you out on a date. I mean, like, a real one." He looked back at her. "I completely understand if you say no. I mean, this is rather unusual. And honestly, I've never asked a client for her phone number before. Actually, I could lose my job for doing this."

Aisha blinked in shock, but the expression on his face was sincere. She thought about what he was proposing. She had to admit to herself that she'd had a great time with him—even beyond the sex. Greg's charm and intelligence had easily won her over, not to mention his handsome face and chiseled body. But he was an escort. Women paid him to take them out. And to have sex with him.

"I'm sorry." Greg's voice interrupted her thoughts. "Asking for your number was really inappropriate. I should go." He began to get out of the bed.

"No, wait." Aisha touched him on the shoulder. "I'll give you my number. I would love to see you again."

Greg's smile lit up the dim room. "Great."

They both got dressed and exchanged numbers. Greg promised to call the next day; Aisha found herself hoping he would. As she closed the door behind him, she sighed. "I hope I'm not making a big mistake."

Chapter Five

A round 11:00 a.m. the next day, as Aisha pored over a report in preparation for Monday's meeting, her cell phone rang.

"Are you hungry?" The sound of Greg's voice took her back to the previous night's activities. Activities she wanted to repeat.

"I could definitely eat. What are you proposing?"

"Only the best fish and grits in Chicago. Can you be ready in half an hour?"

"Absolutely."

Greg pulled up in front of her building exactly thirty minutes later. The black Audi purred silently as Aisha slid down onto the leather seats. *Nothing is going to fall off this car and go rattling down the highway.*

"Nice car. I didn't notice it last night."

"Thank you." Greg flashed his perfect smile, leaned over and kissed her. "You look beautiful."

His kiss ignited a spark of desire within her, but she suppressed it and simply said, "Thank you. You're looking mighty good yourself." And he was. His jeans fit him perfectly, and his leather jacket and sunglasses were stylish, yet unpretentious. "Where are we going?"

Greg pulled out of the driveway and turned the car west. "Have you ever been to Rita Mae's Cafe?"

"No. I've never even heard of it."

"Well,"—he glanced over at her—"She serves some of the best down-home cooking in the city."

"Okay. I'll be the judge of that. I've had some pretty good meals in my life."

"Ah, but you haven't had Rita Mae's. You'll love it." As the car cruised through the city, Aisha and Greg laughed and joked about music, movies and politics. The lake fell away behind them, and the tall high rises were replaced by red brick six-flats and quiet bungalows as they drove through the empty Sunday afternoon streets. Aisha was having so much fun she barely noticed when Greg stopped the car.

"Are we here?" The street was lined with abandoned buildings and dilapidated cars.

"We are." They got out, and in front of them stood a small, storefront restaurant. The name "Rita Mae's Cafe" was scrawled in black marker on a poster board perched at an angle in the window. Greg opened the door for her and they stepped inside. Almost every table was filled. Laughter and loud, joyous conversations bounced off the walls, and the smell of bacon, biscuits and other deliciousness wafted through the room.

"Hey, sugar." The woman at the front counter greeted Greg. "I didn't see you last week. What you been up to?"

"Oh, I had to work, LaDonna. How've you been?"

"Good." She glanced briefly at Aisha. "Morning's been busy, as usual, but I think your table is available."

"Great."

LaDonna weaved her way through the tightly packed tables and led them to a small, rickety metal two-seater by the window. She placed the menus down in front of them. "Enjoy."

"Thanks," Greg replied. He took off his jacket and hung it on the back of his chair. His short sleeve maroon T-shirt showed off his muscular arms and his broad chest. Aisha found herself hungry for more than just food. "Everything is good here, but I highly recommend the fish and grits."

"That sounds good to me." Aisha scanned the laminated card. The menu was not extensive, but it did hit on the down-home favorites—biscuits and gravy, pancakes, ham and eggs. Aisha's mouth watered. "How did you know about this place?"

"I grew up not far from here. We've been coming here since I was a kid."

"Ah, so you're from the West side."

His eyes twinkled. "I am. Is that a problem?"

"Nope. I have no problem with that."

"Hey, Greg! Missed you last week." The waitress, a woman in her fifties, grinned broadly at him.

"Yeah, I had to work. Patrice, this is Aisha. Aisha, Patrice."

"Nice to meet you, honey." She winked at her. "It's nice to finally see Greg in here with someone. He's too damn good looking to be eating by himself all the time. The usual?"

"Yes, ma'am, and make it two please." He smiled at Aisha. "Trust me, you'll love it."

Patrice scribbled the order down on her pad. "Coffee?"

"Yes, please."

"All right." Patrice shoved the pad into the front pocket of her apron. "I'll be right back."

"Thanks, Patrice," Greg said as she walked away. He turned back to Aisha. "So, am I to assume, then, that you're a South sider?"

"You would be assuming correctly. Is that a problem?"

"No. Just so long as you don't think that everyone from the West side is a thug and a gangbanger."

"Ha! No, I don't think that. The South side definitely represents when it comes to thugs and gangbangers. In fact, I think we were the only ones on my block to actually graduate from high school."

"I hear that." Patrice returned with their coffee. Aisha watched the fragrant steam rise from her mug. She took a sip and found it strong and delicious. "You don't take anything in your coffee?" Greg asked.

"No, I like it black." Greg raised one eyebrow. Aisha paused, the mug halfway to her lips, and laughed. "Okay, insert really bad sexual joke here."

Greg chuckled. "Hey, I didn't say anything."

"You didn't have to. Your face said everything." Her cell phone buzzed, and she reached into her purse and pulled it out. The email icon was flashing. "Excuse me for one second."

She tapped the screen and a message from Bill popped up. "Do you have any numbers for a fifteen-second spot?" it read. Aisha smiled slightly and typed a quick response. "Yes. I'll email another rate sheet to you shortly." She hit send and dropped her phone back into her purse.

"Sorry about that. A client."

"Contacting you on a Sunday?"

"Yes, I'm trying to convince him to add a few TV spots to his ad campaign." She picked up her mug and took another sip.

"Do you think he will?"

"Yes, I do. I can be rather...persuasive."

"I see." His full lips curled upward before taking another sip. "A woman who knows what she wants and goes after it." He winked. "Very sexy."

"What can I say?" They locked eyes for a moment. Her phone rang, and she pulled it back out. It was Tanya. Aisha sent the call to voicemail and turned the ringer off. She'd give her the full report later.

"Boyfriend this time?"

She snorted. "No. Actually, it was my friend who hooked me up with your...um...company."

"Ah. And now she's calling you for the morning after play-by-play."

Aisha smirked. "Yeah. Something like that."

"Well, I hope the report is favorable."

"It most definitely is."

"Here you go." Patrice set down two plates overflowing with fried catfish filets and piping hot grits.

"Wow, this looks great." Aisha grabbed the butter and put some on her grits. "You may have been right in your assessment of the food in this establishment."

"Oh, I was right." Greg sprinkled hot sauce on his fish. "Best kept secret in town. I'm telling you."

The fish flaked easily under her fork, and when she took a bite, the crispy, spicy flavor surprised her.

"Good?"

"Fantastic. Hey,"—Aisha sipped her coffee before continuing—"I wanted to thank you for saving my ass last night with your whole culinary school thing. I hadn't come up with any cover story. So thanks."

"It wasn't a story."

Aisha raised her eyebrows. "You really were an investment banker?"

"Yes."

"And you really went to culinary school?"

"Yes."

Aisha paused. "Wow."

"What? Is that so hard to believe?"

"Oh, no." Aisha leaned forward. "It's just that—"

"Greg, baby!" The greeting of a tiny woman cut Aisha off. Her white hair was pulled back into a sloppy bun and covered in a hairnet. She extended her thin arms. Greg stood up, leaned down and hugged her gently.

"Hey, Auntie Rita."

"We missed you last week." Her watery eyes looked at him affectionately.

"I know. I've been hearing it from everyone. I had to work last week."

Rita patted Greg on the side of his face. "You work too much, baby. You need to take it easy every once in a while."

Greg grasped Rita's boney hand and squeezed it between both of his. "I've been saying the same thing to you for ages. When are you going to retire?"

Rita took her hand back and smoothed down the front of her apron. "Now you know I can't retire. I got no one to take over the restaurant. I've told you that."

Greg sighed. "I know. Still, I wish you'd take it easy. Go on a vacation or something."

Rita laughed sharply and looked at Aisha. "Who's your friend, baby?"

"This is Aisha. Aisha, this is Rita Mae Parsons. She's the culinary genius behind that great dish you are eating."

"Pleased to meet you, Ms. Parsons. The food is delicious."

"Oh please, baby, call me Auntie Rita." She grasped Aisha's hand and squeezed firmly. "Glad you like the food. Eat up. Enjoy yourself. Nice to meet you." Auntie Rita smiled at Greg and patted him on the shoulder before heading back through the restaurant.

"Okay, I'm sold." Aisha continued to devour her breakfast. "This is a great place."

"Told you."

They ate in silence for a few moments. Aisha relished the hearty food and the warm, vibrant atmosphere. The walls were cluttered with an eclectic mix of colorful artwork and framed photographs. Some were of people, and others seemed to be pictures of the neighborhood in better times. Tree-lined streets, immaculately kept lawns, white-washed storefronts and smiling people all hung above the heads of chatty diners. Aisha watched as Auntie Rita circulated, greeting patrons, giving hugs and laughing heartily She sighed.

"Are you okay?"

"Yeah." Aisha smiled. "This is a really great place. Thanks for bringing me."

"You're welcome."

Aisha paused for a moment. She didn't want to ruin the great afternoon, but she had burning questions that she needed the answers to. "Can I ask you something?"

"Sure."

"Do they know?" She gestured around the restaurant. "What you do?"

Greg grinned sheepishly. "Not really. I told them I work for an entertainment company. Since they know I went to culinary school, I think they think I'm a caterer."

"Really?"

"Yeah. I think so."

"What about your family?" Aisha stopped for a moment. "I'm sorry, if that's too personal a question I—"

"No, it's fine. They know. I've been doing it for ten years, so they ought to know."

Aisha's eyes grew wide. She leaned across the table and lowered her voice. "You've been an escort for ten years?"

"Yep. Since I was twenty-five."

Patrice returned to their table. Aisha sat back in her chair. "More coffee?"

"Yes, please." She refilled both of their mugs. Aisha watched her walk away before turning back to Greg. "How does that happen? I mean, how did you—"

"Get started?" Aisha nodded. "I got downsized at my job at the bank. I had student loans I had to pay back, rent I had to pay, and while I was working, I was sending my mom money every week to help her with her bills. I tried to get another banking job, but nothing was coming through." He took a sip from his steaming mug. "I had a friend who worked for them, so he hooked me up." He shrugged. "And that was it."

"Wow." Aisha shook her head. "And that was it."

"Yep."

"So, when did you go to culinary school?"

"When I turned thirty. It was my birthday present to myself." He polished off the last bite of fish. "I've always wanted to be a chef, and by then, I had paid off my student loans and had saved enough to go back to school, so I did."

"So are you going to open your own restaurant?" Aisha finished her food as well. She sat back contentedly.

"Eventually, yes." Greg signaled to Patrice for the check. "I plan on quitting the escort business and opening my own place. I'm just waiting for the economy to get better. Now is not the right time to open a restaurant."

"You've got that right. The few restaurant clients that are still on our books have dropped their advertising budget down to almost nothing."

"Don't be a stranger next week, honey." Patrice tore the slip of paper off her pad and set it down on the table. She then winked at him. "And be sure to bring your friend back with you."

"Oh, I plan to." Greg's face lit up. "If she'll join me, of course."

Aisha smiled. "Of course."

Greg paid the bill on the way out, and they got back in his car and headed to Aisha's apartment.

Chapter Six

O nce in front of her place, Aisha invited Greg up. He answered her invitation with a slow, sensual smile.

"Your view is even more stunning during the day." Greg inhaled the warm spring air as they stood out on her balcony. From fifteen stories up, the crystal blue lake looked endless. Underneath them, shrunken cars whizzed by on the Drive, and to the left the skyline glittered in the sun.

Aisha watched the water gently churning, the small waves sparkling. "Yeah, it is nice."

Greg's eyebrows pinched together in a small frown. "What's the matter?"

"Oh, nothing. It's just something that my friend said about my place."

"What did she say?"

Aisha leaned against the balcony, facing him. "She said it was intimidating. To men. My apartment. This view." She tilted her head slightly. "Is it?"

Greg took a step closer to her. The breeze gusted around them. "To some men, maybe, but not to me." He put his hand on her hip and squeezed firmly.

Aisha leaned into him, and her heart raced in anticipation of where he might touch her next. "And why not to you?"

Greg ran his fingers down her cheek. "Because I like women who have their own thing. Who are successful in their own right. It's very sexy. Besides,"—he grinned—"I'm going to be a big-time chef one day, and I'm going to need a woman who can hold her own." He then pulled her close, leaned down and kissed her. His soft lips pressing against hers started the delicious familiar tingle between her legs.

"Shall we get more comfortable?"

Greg answered her by allowing Aisha to lead him back inside. Once in the bedroom, she grabbed Greg and kissed him hungrily. He returned her kisses with equal enthusiasm, further igniting Aisha's passion. She reached down, undid his pants and wrapped her hand around his firm cock. He groaned and unzipped her jeans.

"Take it all off. Now," he commanded.

Without hesitation, she threw off her shirt, took off her jeans and her shoes, unhooked her bra and slipped her panties to the floor. In an instant, Greg was naked as well. His flawless brown skin flexed and moved over his tight, muscular body.

Greg grabbed Aisha around the waist and forcefully pulled her against him. She practically bounced off his solid frame. "So how many orgasms would you like this time?" his voice rasped in her ear. He bent down and kissed her neck, and she wrapped her arms around him and raked her fingers across his back.

"Two is good." Her pussy ached for him.

"Two it is, then." She lay down on the bed, and he pounced on top of her, his hands revisiting all the places they had the night before. Cupping her left breast, Greg brought it to his lips. He consumed a mouthful, sucking and teasing her nipple, and the sensation made her gasp. He released her left breast and moved over to her right one, doing the same, and her pussy screamed for the attention her breasts were receiving. Aisha gripped Greg's shoulders and guided him downward. She had to have him lick her again. The mere thought of his warm tongue caressing her folds made her squirm in anticipation. He gave way a few inches in obedience to her unvoiced demand before stopping and looking up at her.

She met his gaze. "What?"

"Nothing. I'm just getting the feeling that there is something specific you want me to do."

"There is."

"Really, now." He circled her bellybutton with the tip of his tongue. She half giggled and half shuddered. "And what is that?"

"I want you to continue using that tongue of yours. Except,"—she pressed down on his shoulders again—"keep going just a few inches lower."

"Oh really?" Greg popped his head up. Aisha twitched in frustration. "But what if I don't want to do that?"

"What do—"

"What if I'd rather do this?" He slid two of his fingers inside her, and Aisha arched her back, gasping in shock and pleasure. He slowly glided his fingers around and around inside her, pressing gently along her wet inner walls. "Let me see now," he whispered as he continued exploring. "Where is it?"

"W-what are you looking for?" She struggled to ask the question. Greg's fingers hit upon a particular spot inside her, and a new sensation crept up her back and into her shoulders—like thousands of tiny electric pinpricks. She groaned, her hips pressed into the bed and her head buried itself into the pillow.

"Found it." From far away, Aisha could hear Greg's voice, but it was being filtered through a haze of static that had worked its way up into her skull. Her pussy overflowed with wetness, and Greg's fingers moved effortlessly inside her. He rubbed her internal spot faster, and Aisha's hands flew up to her head when she came, as if the force of the orgasm would cause it to explode. Overwhelmed, Aisha couldn't speak, and she flopped around involuntarily as the orgasm continued to ripple up and down her body. She grew dizzy from lack of air and forced herself to inhale deeply.

"Stop." Her command was weak and breathy. "Please."

Greg removed his fingers, and Aisha shuddered. "That's one." Greg's voice was more audible now, but she still had a hard time concentrating on it over the sound of the blood rushing in her ears. After what felt like several minutes, she gained control of her body again and opened her eyes. Greg lay next to her, an amused expression on his face.

"What?"

"Nothing. I'm just giving you a chance to recover from number one before we move on to number two."

"No." Aisha shook her head in futility. "One's good. I'm good."

"Oh, no." He wrapped his arm around her and pulled her close to him. "You know the rules. Two is the minimum." With her nose pressed up against his chest, Aisha could smell the lingering remnants of his soap and cologne. She ran her fingertips lightly over his rich brown skin, and his cock twitched and slowly began to rise. Aisha watched it grow in response to her caresses, expanding in length and girth. She ran her hand down the contours of his flawless body. Smooth skin gave way to rough hairs as she reached the base of his cock. She wrapped her hand around it, barely covering the surface. She tugged gently, and he inhaled sharply, burying his face into the side of her neck.

"How does that feel?" she whispered.

"Good," Greg grunted. "Don't stop." She loosened her grip and ran her hand up and down its entire length, slowly at first and then more quickly. Greg's breathing increased in response to her rhythm.

"Like that?" His hot breath tickled her skin, and in response, she stroked him faster. "Do you like that?" She punctuated her question by nibbling on his ear.

"Yeah." The word came from the back of his throat, and it inspired Aisha to keep going. She rubbed her thumb over the tip of his cock, smearing the wetness that had escaped. When she stroked it hard from tip to base and cupped his balls, Greg grunted.

"Condoms. I need to get my condoms."

He shifted to get up, but Aisha grabbed his solid shoulder. "Drawer." She gestured to the nightstand. "I have some in the drawer."

He scooted up, reached across her and got a condom out of the nightstand. In a flash, he ripped it open and put it on. "Stand up." He jumped out of the bed and pulled her to him. He then grabbed the back of her neck and kissed her fiercely before turning Aisha around, bending her at the waist so she leaned down on the bed and entering her.

Aisha practically screamed when he rammed his cock inside her. He moved his hips slowly at first, coming in and out of her with a smooth rhythm. She grew wetter, and he squeezed her hips firmly, increasing his speed. With one foot, he spread her legs wider and penetrated her deeply. She whimpered, and the sound of her pleasure seemed to excite him. In an effort to give him as much pleasure as he gave her, Aisha arched her back, and she could feel his grip tightening in response. He pounded her faster and faster before slipping one hand between her legs and rubbing her clit gently.

Aisha screamed when the orgasm hit her. He rubbed her clit faster and slammed himself inside her furiously. Orgasm number two coursed up and down her body, and her knees grew weak, unable to support her weight anymore. Just before she thought she'd collapse, Greg came, his body shaking. After a few moments, he stepped away from her, panting. Aisha finally fell down on the bed, and he lay beside her.

Her body was covered in sweat. She took a few deep breaths and sighed.

"Number two."

"Number two." Aisha exhaled. "I don't believe it, but there was a number two. Again."

"Well, I do aim to please."

"And please you do." She put her hands underneath the pillow and turned to face him. "Mmm. Thank you."

Greg rolled over on his side; they were so close their noses almost touched. "You're welcome. Although, I should be thanking you as well."

"Well then, you're welcome." Greg kissed her lightly on her lips. Aisha's heart fluttered.

"Hey, can I ask you a question?"

"Sure."

"How is it that a beautiful, successful woman like yourself doesn't have a boyfriend?"

"I don't know. I did have one, but it didn't work out. My friend Tanya thinks that I'm a workaholic, perfectionist, control freak who intimidates most men and who ends up going out with a string of losers so I don't actually have to get emotionally involved."

Greg raised his eyebrows. "And is that true?"

"I don't know." Aisha rolled over to her back and contemplated the ceiling. "Maybe it is. Some of it. I don't know." The bright afternoon sun streamed in through the window and cast cheery patterns on the wall. "One thing I do know is that I'm damn good at my job, and the workaholic thing is true. I'll own up to that. I've worked hard to get where I am, and—"

"And you deserve everything you have as a result of that hard work." Greg gently touched her arm.

She glanced at him. "Do you really think so?"

He pulled her close. His delicious scent radiated off of his naked body. Aisha closed her eyes and inhaled. "Absolutely. And any guy who would be intimidated by your success is an insecure asshole who wouldn't know a good woman if she walked into the room naked and handed him a beer." Aisha laughed. "I'm serious, Aisha. You're a good woman, and you deserve all of your successes."

"And what about the other stuff? The control freak? The dating losers?"

Greg stroked her hair. "Well, you did a pretty good job of letting me run things a few minutes ago." He kissed her forehead.

"Mmm, and you certainly did run things."

"And I know for damn sure I'm not a loser."

Aisha snorted. "You've got that right. You're the farthest thing from it." She buried her head into his chest again, enjoying his presence—the sound of their soft breathing a perfect complement to the sunny beams scattered across the bed. "And what about you? How is it that a handsome man like yourself is single?"

"Occupational hazard."

"What?"

"It takes a special kind of woman to date an escort." His voice grew low. "I understand it. I mean, I do entertain women for a living." He paused for a moment. "Does my job bother you?"

Aisha looked at his handsome face, his brown eyes staring deeply into hers. "You know, I've been thinking about it. And I don't think so." She trailed her fingers down his smooth chest, watching it rise and fall to his steady breathing. "I'm actually surprised. I mean, perhaps it should." She looked back at him. "But it doesn't."

"Good. Because this is my job. It's what I do for a living, how I pay my bills, and I want you to understand that before we get in this any further. I've been doing this for a long time, and my entire family knows it and accepts it. If we're going to see where this thing goes, I need to know you accept it as well.

Aisha could see the earnestness flashing in his eyes. "I do. I do accept it."

"Okay good. Remember, it's just a job. I don't get emotionally involved with my clients."

Aisha smirked. "Not even with me?"

Greg grinned and took her hand, entwining her fingers with his own. She lay her head back down on his bare chest. "Well, you're no longer my client, now are you?"

She could hear his heart beating a slow, steady rhythm. "I guess I'm not."

Chapter Seven

"**M**y God, I've been calling you forever." Tanya sounded exasperated on the other end of the phone. "Where have you been? How did it go? Did you get some ass last night? Details, woman! I need details!"

Aisha laughed. "Okay, so before I say anything, I just want to thank you."

"For what?"

"For what? For hooking me up." Fresh from the shower, Aisha stretched out on her patio chair, her face tilted toward the warm sun.

"So it went well, I take it?"

"Mmm. Very well."

"Stop teasing me, Aisha! Give me the details. Who did they hook you up with?"

"Greg. Greg Williams." The sound of his name made Aisha smile.

"Hmm. I've never had him. Was he fine?"

"Only the finest man I've seen in a long time."

"I told you," Tanya squealed. "Did you bone? How was his body? Was he hung?"

"Yes. Fantastic. Yes."

"Oooh, girl. That's what I'm talking about." Tanya chuckled. "That must have been some good dick, too, because you still sound relaxed even today."

"Well, I am relaxed, considering he just left about thirty minutes ago."

"What? He spent the night? Damn, how much did that cost you?"

"Nothing." A refreshing breeze washed over her. "He went home last night, but this morning he picked me up and we went out to breakfast. Have you ever heard of Rita Mae's Cafe?"

"No." Tanya paused. "Wait. Are you saying you went out with him again this morning?"

"Yep. The restaurant is this little place on the West side. It looks completely broken down from the outside, but the food was fantastic. Greg knows Auntie Rita. He grew up going to the restaurant as a kid. Oh, and he's a chef. He went to culinary school, and he wants to open his own restaurant one day, but he's waiting—"

"Wait," Tanya interrupted her gushing. "He took you out to breakfast?"

"Yes."

"And you didn't pay for it?"

"No. It was a real date. I didn't pay for his company or anything."

Tanya paused. "Oh, no, girl."

"What?"

"He's an *escort*. You can't date him."

"Why not?"

"Why not?" Tanya sounded incredulous. "Because he's an *escort*. He fucks women for a living. And they pay him. I hate to sound harsh, but that makes him a prostitute. A very fine, very hung, chef prostitute. But a prostitute just the same. And you can't date a prostitute."

"Stop calling him a prostitute."

"But he is."

"No, he's not."

"Aisha." Tanya sighed. "Okay, think of it this way. How many years has he been a pros— an escort?"

"Ten."

"Ten? Damn!" Tanya groaned. "Then he's had sex with thousands of women. Thousands! Do you want to date someone like that?"

"So? I don't care about the number. Half the men on the street have slept with thousands of women and have the babies to prove it."

"And I wouldn't want you to date them either." Tanya's volume increased. "Does he have any children?"

"I don't know."

"Well, don't you think that's something important to know?"

"Yeah, but I'll find that out eventually. Besides, it wouldn't matter."

"Even if his baby momma is a former client?"

Aisha paused. "No."

"You don't sound convinced."

"Look, I know this thing doesn't make any sense. But I don't know, I'm really feeling Greg." She looked out at the rippling lake. With not a cloud overhead, the water and the sky formed one expanse of blue. "I just gotta go with this one. See how it plays out."

"Well, for the record, I think this is a terrible idea, and I hope you don't get your feelings hurt."

Aisha hoped she didn't get her feelings hurt as well.

Chapter Eight

Greg set the tray down in front of her. The fragrant steam rose from the crusty Panini, the melted cheese oozing down the sides. On the tray also sat a small plate heaped high with potato chips and a bowl of strawberries with a mountain of whipped cream. A beer fresh from the fridge was squeezed in the corner, and the beads of perspiration ran down its long neck and formed a small pool of water on the tray.

"This looks fantastic." Aisha sat up and pushed the rumpled sheets to the side. Greg's discarded T-shirt lay in a heap on the floor by the bed, and she grabbed it and put it on before turning back to her lunch. "Did you do all of this just now?"

"Yeah, it was easy. These don't take very long to make."

Aisha picked up the sandwich and took a bite. The flavors exploded in her mouth. "What's in this?"

"It's just a grilled chicken breast, spinach and some goat cheese. Oh, and a homemade raspberry dijon mustard."

"That you just whipped up." Aisha took another bite.

Greg chuckled. "Well, yeah. I am a chef, you know."

"And what about these?" Aisha held up a potato chip. "Did you just whip these up, too?"

"No." Greg took one off of her plate and ate it. "Those I bought. But next time, I can make the potato chips too, if you'd like."

"Yeah, you know, you really should do that because clearly you're slipping on this whole lunch thing." Aisha tried to keep herself from smiling. "I mean, how could you even think to serve me potato chips from a bag?" She ate one. "Oh, hold on. These are Snaps. My favorite. I'll let the whole potato chip thing slide. This time."

"You like Snaps too? Best potato chip on the market, especially the barbeque ones."

"I love those." Aisha took a sip from her ice cold beer. "You know, I grew up not far from the factory. Some days you'd go outside and the air would smell like potato chips."

"Really?"

"Oh, yeah." Aisha took another big bite from her rapidly disappearing sandwich. "There was nothing better than going down to the corner store on a sunny summer day—the air smelling like frying potatoes—and getting a bag of Snaps and a grape pop."

"You like the grape? I liked the strawberry."

"Your store had the strawberry? That's fancy. Ours never did. Only grape and orange." Greg scooted up next to her on the bed, making himself comfortable by propping pillows against the headboard. Shirtless, his ab muscles flexed and contracted with every move. Aisha's sandwich now gone, she picked up the beer and leaned back. Her shoulder pressed up against his. "This was great. Thanks for convincing me to play hooky for a few hours."

"Well, you work too hard." He nudged her affectionately. "You need to take a break every once in a while."

The cool bubbles tickled their way down her throat as she took a sip from the bottle. "I have to work hard."

"Why?"

"Why? Because I've got bills to pay."

"So let's say you pay all of those bills." Greg put his arm around her. "Then what would you use your money for?"

Aisha pondered Greg's question for a moment. "Shoes." Greg laughed. "And clothes, and purses. Oh, and to get my hair and nails done every week. And then to go on vacation." She paused. "I'm sure I can come up with some other stuff if I think for a few minutes.

"Well, it's a good thing you at least have a plan for your money."

"No, really, in all seriousness, I don't know what I'd do. I work because don't know what else to do. As Tanya correctly points out, I've got a problem."

"You're ambitious."

"I am." She paused, remembering sunny summer days, air ripe with the smell of potato chips, and grape pop. "I think it's because I grew up around people who weren't, so I felt like I had to be doubly ambitious to make up for everyone else."

"I understand that." Greg grabbed another chip. "But money should be used for something. It should have a purpose."

"Like for going to culinary school?"

"Like for gong to culinary school."

"So tell me about that." She finished the last sip of beer and placed it back down on the tray. "When did you first know you wanted to be a chef?"

"Oh ever since I can remember. My mom is a great cook, and I always helped her in the kitchen."

"You did?" Aisha snuggled closer to Greg and put her head on his bare shoulder. The curtains billowed as the spring breeze wafted in through the open windows in Greg's master bedroom. The office could wait a little while longer. "What's her best dish?"

"Her seafood gumbo, hands down."

"Really?"

"Absolutely. When my mother makes her gumbo, all the neighbors, all the relatives, people you don't like, people who normally wouldn't give you the time of day, suddenly show up with a bowl and a spoon." Aisha laughed. "It would make me so mad that all these people would just show up, eat my mother's food, and leave, but she always told me if there was anything on the stove, people were welcomed to it."

"Your mother sounds like a great woman."

"Oh, she is." Greg reached over and picked up the spoon on Aisha's tray. "Speaking of food, try this." He scooped up some strawberries and whipped cream and fed it to her. The berries had been soaked in something, and the sharp liqueur contrasted perfectly with the sweet berries and the smooth whipped cream. She looked at him. "It's cognac."

"So delicious."

"Well, in the absence of a concentration in desserts and pastries, I do what I can."

Aisha took the spoon from him and helped herself to another bite. "What do you mean?"

"Learning how to cook desserts and pastries is a whole other set of skills, and you can do a concentration in culinary school. I chose not to because I want to eventually run a restaurant that serves down-home cooking, so all I need to know how to make are the basics—peach cobbler, sweet potato pie, bread pudding, that kind of stuff."

Aisha licked the last of the whipped cream off the spoon. "And you know how to make all of that?"

"Absolutely."

She put the spoon back down on the tray and placed everything on the floor before snuggling up against him. "Well why didn't you just go ahead and whip one of those up?" She shook her head slowly. "There you go again, slipping."

Greg's smile turned Aisha's thoughts to having one more quickie before she had to return to the office. "I'll try to do better next time," he whispered, kissing the remnants of the strawberries from her lips.

Chapter Nine

"My God, this is delicious. What is this again?"

"Coq au vin. It's a French dish. Braised chicken prepared with a wine-based sauce."

"This is seriously tasty." Aisha took another sip of her wine from her leaded crystal glass and relished the flavor profiles as they slid over her tongue. "So, exactly how many benefits are there to seeing a chef?"

"Many. And you haven't experienced them all yet."

"Oh, really? There's more?"

"Yes, but you'll have to wait until after dessert to find out."

Aisha continued eating. She looked around Greg's open kitchen in his cozy, North side home. Everything in it from the plates to the rugs on the hardwood floor to the pictures on the walls reflected Greg's love of beauty and simplicity. And many small decorating touches revealed an understated but expensive personal sense of style.

"I'm glad I was finally able to cook a real dinner for you, instead of throwing something together for a quick lunch." Greg's sexy voice washed over her. Aisha contemplated telling him to skip dessert so they could get to those other benefits.

"Me too." She finished her meal and sighed contently. "It's nice to have a dinner date after all these weeks."

"I know. I'm sorry about that. My evenings have been booked up solid. It's good to have a night off."

Aisha said nothing and drained her glass of the last drop of wine. As much as she tried to get used to it, the more she started to care for him, the more talking about Greg's job, even in a general way, made her feel uncomfortable. She changed the subject. "This wine is delicious. What did you say it was again?"

"It's a pinot noir." Greg poured her another glass. "I know you prefer a pinot grigio, but to serve white wine with this dish would be a travesty." He poured another glass for himself. "Salud." Aisha lifted her glass, and Greg slowly touched hers with his. His brown eyes stared at her deeply, and the ping of their glasses ignited her desire. Greg read the look in her eyes. "Shall we move on to dessert?"

"Mmm. Yes, please." She took another sip and relished in watching his bicep flex as he picked up her empty plate. His jeans highlighted everything, and she couldn't peel her eyes off of his ass as he walked over to the sink. She wanted to squeeze it firmly as he entered her. The sudden ring of Greg's cell phone cleared her mind of her dirty thoughts.

"Hello?" Aisha took another sip of her wine and glanced at the fancy grill out on Greg's patio deck. Despite the fact that she was full, her mouth watered at the thought of the fantastic grilled dishes Greg could whip up once the weather really got warm. "Okay, hold on. Let me write that down." He went over to the fridge and uncapped the pen attached to the whiteboard stuck there. "Six o-clock. Khaki and white. Where? Oh, I've been there before. Right. Thanks." He hung up the phone and smiled awkwardly. "Sorry about that."

Aisha shrugged. "No problem."

"Now." Greg smiled his perfect smile "Where were we? Oh, yes. Dessert." He went to the counter and began preparing the crème brûlées.

"So, um, you have to work tomorrow?"

Greg kept his back to her as he sprinkled them with sugar. "Yeah." He paused. "Unfortunately." He turned on the torch gun and ran it back and forth over the ramekins for a few seconds. He then placed the perfectly browned dishes on the table in front of her. "We should wait about five minutes before we eat them. Do you want some coffee?"

"No, the wine is fine, thanks." Behind Greg's shoulder, Aisha could see the specs of the next assignment glaring at her. She forced herself to turn away. Greg stared at her pointedly. "So,"—she took another sip—"where do you have to go?"

"Uh, the Yacht Club." He picked up his spoon and tapped the top of his brûlée. "Which is actually not good because I kind of get a little sea sick, and the food on those boats is often terrible. I think this is ready. Shall we try it?"

"Yeah, okay." Aisha broke into her dessert. It looked delicious, but she really couldn't taste anything. Her eyes kept fixating on the fridge—6:00, khaki and white.

"You know what?" Greg got up from the table and went over to the whiteboard. He erased it with one swipe of his hand. "I'll put this in my calendar." He picked his phone off the table, typed it in and sat back down. "How's your dessert?"

"It's good." Aisha forced herself to take another bite. "Almost as good as your chicken."

"Thanks." Greg suddenly reached across the table and took her hand. "You would tell me if something bothered you, right?"

"Yes. I would."

He looked at her skeptically. "It's just a job." She could hear the attempt at reassurance in his voice. "Besides, the client tomorrow is an almost fifty-year old woman who spends too much time at the plastic surgeon's and the tanning salon. She just wants someone on her arm so she can make all her friends jealous and maintain her status as some kind of society lady."

Aisha's curiosity surprised her. "Really? You've been out with her before?"

Greg took another bite of his brûlée. "A couple of times. She's always dragging me to these high-society country club functions where she wears way too much makeup and clothes that are all kinds of inappropriate just so she can sit around with her rich friends and bitch about how a black president ruined the country."

Aisha's eyes grew wide. "And what do you do the whole time?"

He shrugged. "I sit there, listen and pretend to be a card-carrying Republican."

"No way. Get out of here. Seriously?"

"Absolutely. What else can I do except tolerate her thinly veiled racist remarks while she tries to grab my dick under the table?"

Aisha laughed so hard tears formed in her eyes. "Greg! You can't be serious. She does that? What do you do?"

"I take her hand and put it back in her lap. Sometimes, especially when she's had a few too many gin and tonics, I make excuses and keep getting up to go to the bathroom. She probably thinks I have a small bladder or a condition or something."

"Oh my God." Aisha wiped away the tears. "So you don't...you know...with her?"

Greg made a face. "Oh, hell no! She always offers. Throws all kinds of money in my face. But no. Absolutely not."

"Oh wow." She took a deep breath. "That's hilarious. Seriously, you could write a book."

"I'm sure I could."

"So, I'm curious." Aisha took another bite of her dessert. She could finally taste the crisp topping and the sweet, creamy custard underneath. "I don't mean to be all up in your business, but you have a really nice house and a really nice car. So I take it your job—and I'm just talking about the above-board stuff—is financially rewarding?"

Greg smirked. "Are you asking me if I make a lot of money escorting?"

Aisha could feel the relaxing effects of several glasses of wine. They had begun to loosen her tongue. "Yes. That's what I'm asking you."

"To be frank, yes. I do quite well. Although,"—he took another sip from his glass—"I'm not one of the top earners."

"Really, who is? I mean, you don't have to tell me his name or anything, but what kind of person is he? He's probably some tall, muscular guy in his twenties, right?"

"Actually, no. Just the opposite. He's a little shorter than I am, average build, and in his sixties."

"What?" Aisha leaned forward in her chair. "You're kidding. In his sixties?"

"Yeah." Greg chuckled. "I don't know how much he makes, but the rumors are that it's over six figures. Well over." Aisha sat back, unable to say anything. Greg continued, "It makes sense. Think of it this way. There's an entire population of retired women who need someone to keep them company as they go about their day. They're not working, and they need someone to talk to while they visit the museums, go out to lunch, attend concerts, what have you. Combine that with the fact that there aren't too many older men on staff at the company, and you have the makings of a very lucrative situation. I hear he's booked up solid for months in advance."

Aisha shook her head. "I don't believe it." She then lowered her voice. "Does he have sex with them?"

Greg laughed. "I don't know. I don't ask him. But I hear he keeps his clients very happy."

Aisha snorted. "Now *he's* the one who should write a book."

"You've got that right."

They were quiet for a moment. Aisha studied him carefully over the rim of her glass. She polished off the rest of her wine and set it back down on the table. Her crème brûlée was gone. And she was ready to move to the *after dessert* dessert.

Greg looked at her thoughtfully. "How was everything?"

"Delicious. Thank you." Aisha slowly got up from her chair and walked over to him. "But now I'm ready for you to show me some of those other benefits you were talking about earlier." She squeezed between Greg's chair and the table, swung her leg over, and straddled him, sitting in his lap.

"Mmm." Greg kissed her neck. Even through the denim, Aisha could feel him growing hard. "Well, we chefs know how to throw down in the bedroom as well as the kitchen."

"Oh, really?" Aisha sighed as he slipped his hands up her shirt and unhooked her bra. Her breasts fell into his hands, and he massaged them. "Show me," she whispered. Aisha could taste the crème brûlée and the wine on his lips, and their luscious sweetness made her want to taste more. She grabbed the bottom of his shirt and forced it up over his head. The sight of his bare chest made her grow wet, and she slowly traced her fingers over the contours of his solid six-pack.

Aisha's touch seemed to be too much for him. He grabbed her and kissed her passionately, stopping only long enough to remove her shirt and bra and throw them to the kitchen floor. He leaned down and teased her right nipple with his tongue until it grew hard. Instinctively, Aisha ground her hips into Greg, feeling his cock straining to escape from his pants. Greg moved his warm mouth over to her left nipple, licking it until it grew hard as well. Unable to take it anymore, Aisha popped up. "Bedroom."

They practically ran upstairs. Once there, Aisha tore off her pants and her underwear. All of it had grown uncomfortable as her pussy had gotten wetter. She lay down, and Greg, now naked, lowered his powerful body on top of hers.

He stroked her hair. "Shall we go for the trifecta this time?"

"The trifecta?" Aisha kissed his bottom lip, nibbling on it with her teeth. "What's that?"

"Three orgasms," he whispered, trailing his hand down the side of her body, stopping at her ass to grab it firmly and to grind his hips into hers.

"Mmm." Aisha could feel his hardness teasing her pussy. "I don't know if I can take three. Two may be my limit."

"Oh, I do love a challenge." Greg parted her lips with his tongue and kissed her deeply.

As he explored her body with his lips, teeth, tongue and hands, Aisha buried herself deep into the comfortable bed and enjoyed the experience. Greg began his downward journey, and she gripped the sheets in anticipation of his licking and savoring her waiting pussy. He teased her at first by parting her lips with his fingers and blowing on her gently.

"That tickles!"

"Oh, really? What about this?" Greg fluttered her clit with the tip of his tongue. Aisha moaned.

"So good."

"And this?" He penetrated her with her tongue. She sucked the air in sharply between her clenched teeth.

"Yes."

"And what about this?"

Greg hitched her up with his hands, moved down lower and rimmed the opening to her ass. Aisha jumped back several inches, almost banging her head against headboard. "Hey! What the hell are you doing?"

"What?" Greg blinked. "Don't you like it?"

Aisha could still feel the imprint of his tongue where it circled that sensitive spot. "I don't know." She noticed that her hands were clenched. She made an effort to relax her fingers. "I've never had anyone do that to me before. It felt..." she searched for the right word, "...weird."

Greg propped himself up on one elbow. "You've never had anal before?"

"No." She laughed nervously. "Oh, no. I mean, men have asked...you know...if they can go there, but I've always said no. Nuh uh. No way."

"Come here." He put his hand on her thigh and guided her back down to him. "Let me just try a little something. I won't hurt you. I promise." Aisha raised one eyebrow. The little tongue action was enough to have her jumping out of her skin. She wasn't sure she wanted more. "Trust me, baby. You are going to love this. Besides,"—his gaze moved downward—"your ass looks so good that I can't be down here and not want to do things to it."

The look on Greg's face made Aisha swallow her fear. She slid closer to him. "Okay. I trust you."

"Turn over." Aisha rolled onto her stomach. Greg sat up and massaged both her cheeks with his hands. "Damn, baby." He spanked her once, softly, before continuing to massage her. Aisha looked over her shoulder at him. Greg's eyes were fixated on her butt, his cock hard as a rock.

Feeling brave, she said, "So are you just going to look at it, or are you actually going to do something with it?"

Her question broke his trance. "Hold on a second." He reached over her, opened up the drawer of his nightstand and pulled out a bottle of lube. Aisha eyed it warily. "Don't worry." His words were reassuring. "This will make all the difference."

Aisha faced forward, and she could hear him opening the bottle. She took a deep breath, steadying herself for what might come next. The sheets rustled as Greg moved, and she could feel his breath against her skin as he leaned in closer to her. His tongue teasing her opening again made her jump, but this time, he caught her and held her in place. "Oh no. You're not going anywhere." His words caressed her body, and she tried to relax. He licked her again, and this time, Aisha gave in to the feeling. Tingles danced up and down her spine as Greg's tongue undulated, causing her to groan. The faster Greg's tongue moved, the more her muscles melted, allowing the sensation to flow throughout her entire body. He then pulled back and replaced his tongue with the tip of his finger.

"Take a deep breath, and when I count to three, I want you to exhale. All of it. Blow it all out. Okay?"

"Okay." Aisha found herself quivering in excitement over what was to come next.

"Okay. Ready?"

"Yes."

"Deep breath." Aisha inhaled deeply and could hear Greg doing the same. "One. Two. Three. Blow."

Aisha exhaled, and as she did, Greg slipped his finger into her. She winced at the sharp pain, but moments later, a shock of pleasure formed in the small of her back and radiated down into her pussy. Greg slowly moved his finger in and out. "How does that feel?"

She gasped, barely able to speak. She grunted out one word, "Good," and pressed her face into the pillow, lifting her ass higher in the air. As he explored her tight opening, he took his other hand and spanked her elevated cheek softly. The two very different sensations made Aisha's toes curl. She propped herself up on her hands and thrust her ass back into Greg. "Harder." She hissed through her teeth, "Spank me harder."

Greg obliged, and the sound of the next spank filled the room with a loud pop. Aisha could feel the sweat dripping off her as she rocked her hips. Greg's palm beat out a rhythm that awakened all her senses, and his probing of a newly explored place almost rendered her speechless. Although her entire body trembled with pleasure, she needed Greg to do one more thing. Her pussy was dripping wet and begged for attention.

"Fuck me now." Her voice was low, guttural, gravelly.

"What?"

Aisha struggled to speak. "Put your dick inside of my pussy now." She hoped she made her instructions clear because she doubted her ability to continue to form coherent sentences.

"Okay, one second." Greg broke contact with her. She could hear him fumbling with the condom, and the tingles at the base of her spine began to fade away. Just when Aisha felt her frustration rise, Greg returned. He reinserted his finger without a warning, and she yelped. "Sorry. Are you okay?"

"Yeah." The erotic warmth massaged her lower back again. "But I won't be if you don't fuck me."

Aisha barely finished her sentence before Greg entered her. She moaned, sitting back forcefully on his cock. He thrust forward to meet her, inserting his finger deeper. Aisha gave herself over to the sensations as Greg continued his rhythm, and after a few minutes, she turned back to look at him. Greg's brow furrowed in concentration, his eyes focused on her ass. Aisha tilted her hips slightly, allowing for deeper penetration, and Greg's gaze flew up to meet hers. She licked her lips slowly, and the look that flashed across his face motivated her to shift her hips even more, hoping to give Greg as much pleasure as she was feeling.

Aisha smiled when his eyes rolled back into his head. "How does that feel?"

"Good." The sound seemed to come from the back of his throat. She threw her hips back again and again, and each time Greg was there to meet her with his hard cock. His rhythm sped up, and her eyes snapped shut as a noise escaped from her. It was thick, low and covered with lust—an expression of the two different, intense and completely complementary feelings that raced through her body.

She could feel her orgasm approaching like an ongoing train. It screeched up her back, through her neck, and into her head while simultaneously exploding between her legs, and up and around her stomach, before flooding down into her toes. She lost the ability to speak, to utter any noise at all. Instead, she simply gasped for air, her chest heaving in and out, her fists curled into tight balls. She collapsed face down onto the bed. Greg removed his finger, grasped her waist, and thrust a few more times before grunting with an orgasm of his own. His body convulsed before collapsing on top of her, wet and sleek with sweat.

Aisha couldn't move. She couldn't even open her eyes, and she could barely breathe. Every once in a while, her body would involuntarily twitch as the aftershocks worked their way out. Greg stayed still as well, his arm weighing heavily across her. The sweat on her brow trickled and rolled down her face, trying to collect itself in the corner of her eye. With much effort, she raised a hand and wiped it away.

"I'm sorry if I hurt you," Greg mumbled into the damp sheets.

"What? You didn't hurt me."

"Okay, good." He remained motionless. "It's just that you cried out when I put my finger back there."

"Oh, you just surprised me, that's all." Her arm was falling asleep, so she rolled over onto her back. Greg readjusted himself as well.

"Was it good?"

Aisha shot him a glance. His eyes were still closed. "Baby, I can't even begin to tell you..." her voice trailed off. Words were inadequate to describe what she had experienced.

"Good because that's number one."

Aisha turned to him. He had opened one eye and was peering at her. After a moment they both laughed.

"You're crazy!" Aisha ran her fingers through her hair in an attempt to unstick some of the strands from her forehead. "That was number one, number two, number three, number four, number infinity!"

"Whew, I'm glad." He tried to wipe the sweat off of his face with his forearm, but his body was covered in it as well. "Because I'm going to have to take a little break before we go again."

Aisha could feel her limbs beginning to come under her control again. "Damn, that was good." The sheets were soaked. "It looks like you're going to have to do laundry."

Greg chuckled weakly. "That's quite all right. I don't mind." The two of them fell silent as they recovered.

"Thank you."

Greg inhaled deeply and exhaled loudly. "For what?"

"For what? For that! For that amazing, amazing technique of yours."

"You're welcome. I'm glad you enjoyed it."

"So what about you?" Aisha snuggled her wet body against his. "I've been trying to give as much as I've been receiving over these past few weeks, but I don't really know if it's been as good for you as it has been for me. What do you like to do in bed? What can I do for you?"

Greg stroked her hair. "Everything you've done has been great. You're so sexy."

"Yeah, but there's got to be something you really like that we haven't done yet."

He paused. "Well..."

"Tell me."

"This is probably going to sound stupid but..."

"But what?"

Greg paused again. "Well, I would like to be surprised."

"Surprised? What do you mean?"

He glanced at her and then looked away. "I don't know. It's hard to explain. It's just that—and I don't want you to feel weird about what I'm about to say—" Aisha shook her head in response. "Okay." He exhaled. "It's just that it's my job to please women, to do things that make them happy. It's all about them. In my private life, every once in a while, I'd like for a woman to take control and do something...surprising." He glanced at her again. "I'm sorry, this doesn't make much sense and kind of makes me sound like an asshole, doesn't it?"

"No. It doesn't. I get it." She snuggled in closer.

"Really?" He took her hand and played with her fingers.

"Yeah." She yawned as sleep began to overtake her. "Just be careful because you might get what you wish for."

Chapter Ten

"Hey." Greg peeked around the door to Aisha's office.

"Hey." She got up from her desk and gave Greg quick a hug. "I didn't know you were coming by."

"Well, I was downtown already, and I know you had your big final interview, so I thought I'd surprise you and see how things went."

"I think it went great. I'll find out if I got the job in a couple of days." Her desk phone rang. "Excuse me for one second." Glancing at the caller ID, Aisha sat down, slipped on her headset and answered the phone. "Aisha Anderson."

"Aisha. This is Bill Weinstein."

"Bill. How are you doing today?"

"Fine. Fine." He sounded much calmer than he did the last time they spoke. "Listen, I want to add on two fifteen-second TV spots to my package."

Aisha tried to contain her enthusiasm. "That's great. You're making a wise choice." She looked up and caught Greg's eye as he walked around her office. He winked and then continued studying the awards propped up in her bookcase. She forced her attention back to her headset. "Would you like them both to run in the evening slots?"

"No. I want to target the AM and the PM audience, so I want to spread them out." He paused. "Do you think that's a good idea?"

"I think that's an excellent idea. You'll be targeting the widest audience possible that way. People who are off work, stay-at-home parents and caregivers, third-shift workers as well as the nine-to-five crowd will all be exposed to your company. With your TV and radio spots, print ads as well as the updated website, you're really poised to take this market by storm."

"Yes, that's what I was thinking. And give Welden and Sons a run for their money."

"Absolutely." Aisha turned to her computer and opened up a few spreadsheets. "I'm going to recalculate your package based on this conversation and send you the file when I'm done. You look it over, sign the revised contract and either email or fax it back to me. After I receive the document, I'll give you a call, and we'll move on to the next step. How does that sound?"

"That sounds great. Thanks, Aisha. I look forward to seeing those new numbers."

"Take care. I'll be in touch." Aisha hung up the phone and removed her headset.

"So...success?" Greg leaned casually against the bookcase.

"Yes." Relief washed over her. "A big success. Adding those TV spots really rounds out his package."

"Which is good for you."

"Which is very good for me."

"Now I see why you have this." Greg gestured toward her Employee of the Year award.

Aisha stood up and walked over to him. The etched glass trophy was slightly dusty. She picked it up and brushed her hand along the top of the frosted edge. "Yes, this was from last year. I somehow managed to pull in some big clients, kept others from leaving for other agencies, and convinced a few to upgrade their existing packages."

"Like you did right now."

Aisha returned the trophy to the shelf. "Like I did right now." Greg said nothing. "What is it?"

"Nothing. You're just..." He touched her arm. Aisha could feel the goose bumps forming and for a moment wished she had the time to take an extended lunch break. Instead of finishing his sentence, Greg smiled. "And these certificates? You have a lot of them."

Aisha tore her gaze from him and glanced at the wall. "If you don't get the big award, they give you those."

"How long have you been working here?"

"Seven years."

"Seven years? Then it's definitely time for them to give you that promotion."

"Well, you'll get no argument from me."

Greg leaned down and gave her a quick kiss before moving away. "That's a great paperweight." He picked up the slightly misshapen colorful ball that sat on her desk.

Aisha pressed her lips together, relishing the brief taste of him. "It's pretty cool, isn't it? My nephew made it for me."

"How old is he?"

"Ten going on twenty-one. I keep telling my sister if she doesn't watch it, he's going to take over. He's already too smart for his own good and tries to run things."

"Yeah, boys will do that."

Tanya's question flashed through her mind. "Hey, do you have any children?"

Greg put the paperweight back down. "No, I don't. I would like to have some one day, though."

She tried to hide her relief. "After you open that restaurant and have the entire city of Chicago talking about your cooking?"

"Absolutely."

Greg stepped closer to her, and the look in his eyes made her wish, yet again, for a long lunch break. Better yet, an early quitting time. Glancing over Greg's shoulder, she could see Phil walking by. He stared at her then at Greg before slowly continuing down the hallway. "You know,"—she looked back at Greg's eager face—"let's get out of here and grab a cup of coffee for a few minutes."

"That would be great."

They walked around the corner to the coffee shop, ordered their drinks and sat down at a table. Aisha took a sip from her paper cup. "So, what have you been up to today?"

"I had to go into the main office and talk to my boss about a few things."

"Hey, where is the office anyway? There isn't an address on the card."

"That's deliberate, and all I can say is that it's downtown."

"Hmm." Aisha made a face. "So it's a secret."

"Yes, it's a secret for obvious r—"

"Greg?" A blonde woman who was passing by stopped abruptly at their table.

"Heather! Hey." Greg stood up and gave her a quick hug before sitting back down again. "How is everything? How are Tina and Kristin?"

"They're great. Actually,"—she glanced at Aisha—"we're getting ready to head back out to the casino again." She paused. "And we'd love for you to join us."

Greg cleared his throat. "Okay. Well, you know how to get a hold of me."

Heather smiled. "Yes. I do." She looked back at Aisha one last time before heading over to another table.

Aisha watched her leave before turning back to Greg. He smiled at her apologetically. "I'm sorry if that was awkward for you. Occupational haz—"

"Excuse me." Aisha got up from her chair. "I have to go to the bathroom."

She burst into the stall and closed the door behind her. Her hands shook, and she could feel the tears threatening to rise to the surface. *Calm down. You know he's an escort.* "A prostitute," Tanya had said. *It's just his job*, she rationalized to herself. *It has nothing to do with you. What we have is personal. Special.* She took several deep breaths to clear her head. She then opened the stall door and ran into Heather.

"Sorry," she mumbled.

"Hey, can I ask you something?" Heather's blue eyes stared intensely into hers. Aisha said nothing, but Heather didn't seem to notice. "How much does he charge for a casual coffee thing?" Aisha didn't respond. "I mean, I never thought about doing that, but that is so perfect." Heather smiled. "A quickie in the middle of the day. I mean, it's got to be cheaper than an evening date, but then again, the pleasure of his company for an entire evening is so..." She sucked her breath between her teeth. "Mmm," she said softly. "Hey." She looked around the empty bathroom before leaning into Aisha. "Did he find your G-spot? I thought that it was just a myth. You know, something that those fashion magazines talk about to sell copies, but when Greg put his fingers inside of me,"—her eyes glazed over at the memory—"at first, I was like, 'okay, this is nice,' but he kept rubbing around in there until he found it..." Her voice trailed off, and she shuddered. Her eyes flashed. "I swear I screamed so hard when I came that I startled the neighbors."

Aisha angrily pushed past her and stormed out of the bathroom. She wiped away the tears that threatened to fall as she blew past Greg and headed for the front door.

"Hey, wait, Aisha," he called after her. She ignored him, pulled open the door and almost ran into several people on the crowded sidewalk. Greg grabbed her arm and turned her around. "What's the matter? What happened?"

"I can't do this!"

"What?"

"My God! Have you fucked half the women in Chicago?" She could see the pain on his face; it made her feel good. "You're nothing but a prostitute! I have no idea what I was thinking. Get away from me." She tore her arm out of his grasp and pushed her way down the sidewalk. The tears made it difficult for her to see where she was going, and she stumbled through the crowd on the way back to her office.

Chapter Eleven

"You were right." Aisha balanced the phone on her ear as she lay on her side in the bed. "I should have listened to you."

"I didn't want to be right, girl." Tanya's voice sounded sympathetic. "And you know you should have punched that bitch in the face, right?"

"For what? She was talking the truth."

"Just on general principle." Tanya chuckled. "And it might have made you feel a little bit better." Aisha said nothing. "Did he try to call you?"

"Yeah, he's been blowing up my phone. Calls and texts. I've been ignoring him."

"Good, it's better this way."

"I know, but..." Aisha couldn't finish her sentence.

"But what?"

"But..." she paused again, "...I miss him. I was really starting to care for him."

"I know. But you'll find someone else."

"When?"

"Eventually."

"And where, Tanya?" Aisha grabbed the phone and rolled over onto her back. She readjusted her bathrobe. "You were right about me. I'm a workaholic loser with no life. I date loser men, and the one I found that I actually seriously fell for I had to buy. What does that say about me?"

"Oh, you're not a loser. I was just teasing you before. A workaholic? Yes. But look, your hard work is about to pay off in a big-ass promotion that carries with it some serious cash. And then you'll be so busy with work you won't even have time to think about Greg."

"Yeah, you're right. I'll focus on my career. That's what I do best anyway. Maybe this time next year I'll be promoted to CEO."

"Girl, yes. Then can't nobody touch you. You would be so fierce. Just don't forget the little people who helped you become the woman you are today."

"I could never, Tanya. I know you've always had my back. Thanks."

"No problem. That's what friends are for."

. . . .

A FEW DAYS LATER, AS Aisha sat at her desk staring at her blank computer screen, Phil stuck his head into her office. "Knock knock."

She looked up. "What's up, Phil?"

He entered, his hands in his pockets. His pale blue eyes quickly assessed Aisha's outfit, and she could see a smirk beginning to form. "I, uh, just wanted to say that you were stiff competition, but I'm really looking forward to working closely with you in the future."

Aisha stared at him. "What are you talking about?"

"Oh, you haven't heard?" The smirk made its full appearance. "I got Vicki's job. I really hope there's no hard feelings. Because I know if we work together, this upcoming quarter can be very lucrative for the both of us."

All of the light and the sounds in the room disappeared, and Aisha's mouth went dry. Her heart pounded in her chest, and the only thing she could focus on was Phil's mouth—his thin lips fashioned into a sneer and the occasional flash of yellowed teeth. His lips moved, but she couldn't hear any sound beyond the whoosh of blood in her ears.

"...told me this morning...sure he informed you...tell you this way...forward to working together..."

As though under someone else's control, Aisha got up from her desk, pushed past Phil and walked down the hall to her boss's office. Without knocking, she opened Rob's door and entered. He was on the phone. She barely noticed.

"You gave the job to fucking Phil?"

Rob simply stared at her, his eyes wide. "I'll call you back," he mumbled quickly into the phone and hung up. "Aisha, sit down, please."

"No! You gave the job to fucking Phil? When the hell were you going to tell me?"

"Aisha!" Rob scurried from behind his desk and closed the door to his office. "Keep your voice down, please."

"No! I can't believe this shit! I brought in the most clients last year. Hansen wouldn't have done half as well as it did in this economy without me. Edward even acknowledged me at the damn gala, and you promote fucking Phil?" Aisha felt like she was going to pass out. Her hands shook, and the entire room became bathed in red.

"We promoted the person we thought would be best for the position," Rob said calmly. His deeply lined face betrayed no emotion. "Now you need to calm down, Aisha, and go back to your office."

"No! I will not calm down! This is some bullshit! You can take my office and shove it up your ass. I quit!" She threw the door open so hard it slammed up against the wall. Her coworkers loitered in the hall as Aisha breezed past them. She stormed into her office, grabbed her purse from the coat rack, and went back toward the door. Before leaving, she paused for a moment, returned to her desk and picked up her nephew's paperweight. She then strode back into the hallway, slammed her office door behind her as hard as she could and headed toward the elevators.

Chapter Twelve

By the time she got home, she had gone through all of the tissues she had stuffed in her purse.

Everything she had worked for was gone. The company she had dedicated years of her life to had screwed her over, and she now had nothing. These thoughts raced through her mind as she lay face down on her bed. Her head hurt, her heart hurt, and she knew that after some time, her wallet was going to hurt too. She figured it wouldn't be long before she lost her condo and her car and had to file for bankruptcy. She didn't know what she was going to do. And she didn't have the energy to think about it or to even care.

She wanted to call Tanya and tell her, but the mere act of pulling her phone out of her purse seemed overwhelming. So she continued to lay there, fully dressed, still wearing her heels, her makeup smearing the pillowcase. Finally, she drifted off to sleep, exhausted from the spectacle of the day. Aisha had no idea how long she slept, but the muffled ring of her cell phone awakened her. She sat up and rubbed her eyes, getting mascara on her fingers, before stumbling over to her purse and taking out her phone. She answered it without paying attention to who was calling.

"Hello?" She croaked with a voice still hoarse from the crying.

"Aisha, what's wrong?"

Her heart thudded in her chest at the concern in his voice. "Greg?" Aisha felt a flood of emotion—anger, sadness, affection, relief. "I didn't get the promotion, and I quit my job." She couldn't stop the words from spilling out. "I can't believe they gave it to Phil. Fucking smarmy-ass perverted Phil whose numbers paled in comparison to mine. They gave him *my* job. And then they didn't even have the nerve to tell me I got passed over for that asshole, and I had to hear it from that mother fucker's mouth as he stood there smirking at me, enjoying it and thinking he's going to have a lot of fun being my boss and making my life miserable and uncomfortable. And Mandy told me the reason Vicki left was because of some kind of 'good old boys' club, but I didn't listen to her. She tried to tell me. I should have listened. And so I told the vice president off. I went into his office and told him off and quit and walked out." She stopped talking and the words were replaced by half sobs. She covered her mouth with her hand, but she couldn't stop the tears.

"I'll be there in fifteen minutes."

* * * *

AISHA HUGGED GREG AS soon as she opened the door. His strong arms surrounded her, and she buried her head in his chest. He led her to the couch and held her as she sobbed, silently stroking her hair and rubbing her back. After several minutes, Aisha forced herself to calm down. She took a few deep breaths and looked into his warm brown eyes. "I'm sorry I got your shirt all wet."

He chuckled. She missed that sound desperately. "It's okay. It'll dry." He coaxed her to lean her head back on his shoulder. Several more minutes passed in silence. Greg finally spoke. "You did the right thing."

"Really?" Aisha sat up. "Do you really think so? Or did I just make the most terrible mistake of my life?"

He gripped her hand. "No, you absolutely did the right thing. How can you work for those assholes after this? And I sure don't want you reporting to Phil. I wanted to kill that mother fucker the night of the gala for the way he was looking at you." Aisha couldn't help smiling. Greg stroked the side of her face. "You'll get another job. Don't worry."

She nodded slightly and turned away, suddenly overcome with guilt. "I'm so sorry, baby, for what I said to you. I didn't mean to call you a prostitute. It was bitchy and cruel, and I feel terrible about it."

"Yeah, it was pretty bitchy." His face was serious, but she could see a smile dancing at the corner of his mouth. "You weren't being fair to me. You knew from the beginning what I did for a living. I never hid anything from you."

She exhaled. "You're right. It was so stupid to go off on you. I know your job is to entertain women. I get it, and I'm not going to let it stand between us. I care about you so much and want to be with you."

A small frown formed between his eyes. "Can I ask you something?"

"Sure."

"I saw Heather go into the bathroom after you did. Did she say something to you?" Remembering the conversation, the words stuck in her throat, so she simply nodded. "What was it?"

"S-she,"—Aisha took a deep breath—"she said something to me about your technique in the bedroom. And how much she enjoyed it. I—I couldn't handle it." Fresh tears slid down her cheeks.

"Oh, baby." Greg wiped them away with his thumb. "Don't get upset about that. Even though I did things with other women that I did with you, what we have together is special. I care about you, and that makes it more intimate." His eyes stared deeply into hers. "I never even think about those other women when I'm with you. Ever. When we're together, I make love to you. With those other women, it was just sex. A job. With you, it's different."

"Oh, Greg." She kissed him, and the slow kisses grew more hungry. "I missed you so much." Her heart melted and her desire for him ignited instantly. She reached down to Greg's lap. The feeling of his hard cock under her hands enticed her.

"I missed you too," he whispered.

She groaned as Greg softly bit her neck. They made their way to the bedroom, groping, kissing and undressing all down the hall. By the time they reached the bed, they were both naked, and Aisha sighed when Greg slipped into the bed next to her.

As he kissed her, he ran his hand down the side of her body, stopping momentarily to cup her breast and rub his thumb over her nipple until it grew hard.

"So how many orgasms would you like to have?" Greg's question tickled her ear.

"Actually,"—Aisha pulled back—"that's a question I should be asking you."

"What?"

She leaned into him, making sure to rub her breasts against him as she whispered, "How many orgasms do you want to have?" She wrapped his hard cock in her hand and stroked it from base to tip.

The shock on his face slowly melted into understanding. She moved her hand faster, and Greg grunted. "I think one. One is enough."

"Oh, I don't know." Aisha replaced her hand with her mouth, opening wide so that the tip of his cock touched the back of her throat. Greg groaned. She ran her tongue along the length of his shaft as she sucked her way back to the tip. "I think you've got two of them in you."

Greg's hips bucked, and she clambered between his legs, holding his body down with her hands. "Damn, baby. You're serious about this." His eyes grew wide in anticipation.

"You bet I am." She took him deep into her throat, licking him again as she came up for air. "You're not going anywhere."

Greg arched his back as Aisha consumed him deeply, relishing his salty taste and the hard smoothness of his cock against her tongue. She sucked him slowly at first, and then faster. He touched her hair and stroked it. She used her tongue to caress him, making sure to rim him under the edge of the tip of his cock as she pulled out. Greg's hips moved in tandem with her motion, thrusting himself deep inside her. Aisha heard the tempo of his breath increase, and his hand curled up into a fist, gripping her hair instead of stroking it.

Aisha sucked hard one last time, releasing him with a loud pop. "Oh, no," she said in response to the question in Greg's eyes. "You're not coming yet. It's too soon." She then ran her tongue quickly over his balls. Greg shuddered. "We're just getting started."

Aisha got off of the bed and went over to her closet. Hanging on a rack on the door were several scarves. She took three of them and held them up. Greg raised one eyebrow. "What are you going to do with those?"

"You'll see."

Greg didn't take his eyes off her as she made her way back to him. "Scooch up some," she commanded. Greg obliged, moving closer to the headboard. "Arms up." Greg lifted his arms above his head. Aisha took one of the scarves and tied it around his wrist. She then threaded the other end through one of the slats in the headboard and secured it tightly. She did the same thing with the other scarf before picking up the third.

Greg's eyes glowed with excitement. "Where's that one going?"

Aisha held it up and smiled. "Here." She brought it down around his eyes and blindfolded him. "Can you see anything?"

"No."

"Good." Aisha surveyed his naked, restrained body. His shoulders and pecs flexed in response to the position of his arms, and his abs rippled like a washboard as he breathed. His hard cock jutted upward between his powerful thighs, begging her to do something with it. "Perfect," she whispered.

Aisha bent down and teased his lips with her tongue before kissing him deeply. Greg exhaled as his mouth matched her passion, his arms straining slightly against his restraints. She broke the kiss and nibbled her way down his body, stopping to scrape his nipples with her teeth. Greg made a hissing noise and his abs clenched, his body jerking slightly. "Now you know how I feel." She continued to move downwards and traced the hills and valleys of his abs with her tongue.

Greg jumped. "That tickles."

"Mm hmm. It does, doesn't it?" Aisha flicked the tip of her tongue into his bellybutton and chuckled when he jumped again. Back down at his enticing cock, she took its considerable length into her mouth. Greg groaned when she cupped his balls and sucked hard. She moved her head up and down, each time moving a little faster and making the suction a bit harder. His fingers splayed as he tried to reach out to her.

"You can't touch me," she teased, blowing softly on his balls. His whole body trembled in response to the rush of unexpected air. "Your dick is just too good," she mumbled, her face close to the base, hoping that Greg could feel her words as well as hear them.

"R-really?" he stammered.

"Mm hmm. I have to have more." Aisha reached up into her nightstand and pulled out a condom. She unwrapped it and put it on him. "Do you want to give me more?" She straddled him, positioning her pussy a few inches above his cock.

"Yes." His voice was barely audible.

"I can't hear you."

"Yes," he said, increasing his volume.

"Yes what?"

"Yes, I want to give you more." His arms shook above his head.

"Okay." She sat down hard on his cock, and he moaned and jolted upright, pulling the headboard forward a few degrees. Aisha relished the control she had over the helpless Greg, and she moved her hips in a circular motion watching the veins in his arms bulge to the surface as he strained against the scarves. He attempted to rotate his hips to complement hers, but Aisha kept him guessing.

"Ah ah ah." She leaned down and raked her fingers across his chest, which had grown slick with perspiration. "I'm running the show here." She stopped her circular motion and raised up so only the tip of his dick was inside her. She then sat down swiftly, and Greg's upper body jerked upward again. She continued this pattern for some time—rising slowly to the point of almost coming completely off of him and then taking him hard into her, right up to the base. With each slam, he jumped, and Aisha could see the beads of sweat that streamed down his face.

Gripping him firmly between her thighs, Aisha pounded him furiously. She slipped her hands around his narrow waist for leverage and continued her fast-paced rhythm. She could see the orgasm on his face before it hit his body. Greg's forehead furrowed, and his lips curled upward before grunting loudly—a sound that was sharply cut off by an inhale of breath. His body flopped around like a fish underneath her, and the headboard banged loudly against the wall. Aisha continued to ride him as his flops turned into shakes and then died down to quivers. She finally slowed as the headboard quieted, and Greg's head lolled to one side between his outstretched arms. Aisha got up, removed the condom, and threw it in the trash. She then surveyed him one last time. Greg's feet were splayed in opposite directions, and his cock lay flaccid, exhausted, against his thigh. Loosening the knots, Aisha removed the blindfold and released him from the headboard.

Greg's eyes were closed, his breathing erratic. He brought one hand down to his chest, and the other remained above his head, quivering slightly. Aisha slid up next to his damp body and put her lips close to his ear. "That's one."

Greg laughed weakly. "Damn. One's enough." The words came out in a staggering breath.

Aisha propped herself up on one elbow and watched as his breathing slowly returned to normal. She ran her fingers down his sweaty chest. "Surprising?"

Greg's eyes slowly opened. They were dark pools peering into her. He nodded solemnly. "Yes. Very."

Aisha kissed him gently, and underneath her fingertips, she could feel his heart beating a steady rhythm in his chest. "My job here is done."

A spark lit in his eyes. "Not yet." He then slipped his fingers inside her.

Aisha gasped at the unexpectedness of his move and fell back onto the bed. As he slid his fingers in and out, he rubbed her clit with his thumb. Greg's spontaneity, his technique, and the fact that she could still imagine his cock inside her caused Aisha to come almost immediately. Her orgasm took her breath away. The waves of pleasure surged up to her head and down to her toes as her body shook. She gripped the wet sheets, arched her back and moaned, her hips thrusting upward against her will. Greg continued to rub her, and she clenched her teeth as the sensation became too much.

"Okay." She hissed, "stop!" Greg removed his hand, and Aisha sighed as her pussy pulsated with sensitive energy.

"Good?" he whispered.

"Mm."

"I'll take that as a yes, then."

Aisha lay there listening to the sound of her own heart. Greg pulled her close, and she put her head on his shoulder. "Thank you for that." His voice vibrated in her head.

"You're welcome," Aisha murmured. "Although, I should be thanking you as well. I think we both benefitted."

"I guess you're right."

Aisha lay comfortably in his arms. She thought about the day and everything that had happened. Strangely, at this point, it felt like she'd made the right decision. Somehow, everything was going to be okay.

Aisha let her fingertips dance over Greg's collarbone. "What time is it? Don't you have to go to work tonight?"

"Nope."

"Oh, that's great." Aisha snuggled in closer. "A rare free night."

"Actually, from now on, all of my nights are going to be free."

"What?"

"I said, from now on, all of my nights are going to be free."

Aisha raised up to look at him. "What are you talking about?"

"Well, you aren't the only one who recently quit a job."

Aisha stared at him, trying to comprehend what he was saying. "What? You quit?"

He nodded. "A few days ago." He interlaced his fingers with hers. "Look, I know we haven't been seeing each other long, but I really care about you, Aisha. I haven't been in love for a long time." He sighed. "In fact, I can barely remember the last time, but being with you over these past few weeks has awakened a part of me again—the part of me I had to shut off in order to do my job." He kissed her lips softly. "Now, I can't go back to that life, and I want to find out if I'm still capable of falling in love."

Aisha touched his face. "Oh, baby." She kissed him again. "Why didn't you say anything earlier?"

"Well, because I wanted to make sure you wanted to be with me for me. The guy who entertained women for a living. Because the fact is, that's a part of me, and after ten years, there are thousands of former clients out there. One day we might run into another one and then another one and then another." He raised his eyebrows. "And like Heather, some of them might say something about my technique. Are you going to snap every time that happens?"

"No," she said emphatically. "Absolutely not. What you do...did...for a living is a part of who you are. And I'm crazy about you. Every single part. Besides,"—she smiled—"that *is* how we met, remember?"

"Yes." He pushed a strand of hair away from her face. "It is."

Aisha sighed and lay back down in the crook of his arm. "So, now that we're both unemployed, what do we do now?"

"Well, actually." He smiled slowly. "I have an idea."

Chapter Thirteen

"**I** checked in with Malcolm, and the website will go live in few hours." Aisha ticked the points off on her fingers. "The radio spot will start running next week. I've called my contacts at *The Trib*, *The Sun-Times* and *The Reader* and all three will be sending someone over in the next month or so. They come in stealth mode, so everything at all times has to be perfect—the food, the service, everything. At all times."

Greg cracked several eggs over the griddle and began to scramble them. "It will be, baby. Don't worry."

"I'm serious. A review in the paper can make or break your business. And you really need to talk to Monica. Sometimes she can get a little attitude with the customers."

"I will." He flipped the perfectly scrambled eggs onto the plate, added a few strips of bacon and two fluffy pancakes and set the steaming plate down on the counter. "She's got some stuff going on at home. But I'll talk to her."

"Okay." Aisha pulled out her phone and checked her calendar. "Oh, and the new awning is being delivered tomorrow. And..." she put her hand on her hip, "I really wish you would let me order a new sign. You know, one that isn't handwritten with a marker. The one up there is so...bootleg."

"Absolutely not." Greg wiped his hands on his apron and picked up the catfish filets. He dipped them in milk, dredged them in cornmeal and placed them gently in the hot oil. "That stays. Auntie Rita would kill me if I took it down."

Aisha sighed. "Okay, fine. Oh, and one more thing..."

"What's that?" Greg stirred the large pot of grits and spooned some onto a plate. He added a perfectly fried golden catfish fillet and set the plate down on the counter.

"Would you please come out of the kitchen and talk to people?" Aisha took advantage of the fact that his hands were empty and slid up to him. She wrapped her arms around his waist and pressed her body against his. "They all want to congratulate you for taking over the business and thank you for the amazing food."

He leaned down and kissed her lightly. "But I have to—"

"No buts. Auntie Rita is even out there. Circulating. Talking to customers as usual. She just got back from her Vegas trip, and she wants to tell you all about it. Oh, and my friend Tanya is here, and I want you to finally meet her. We do have her to thank, you know." She winked. "Cliff and Andre can handle things for a few minutes." She looked over at the other cooks. "Can't you, gentlemen?"

"Absolutely. We got this, man." Cliff scurried from one hot burner to another. "Go on and greet your adoring public."

Greg rolled his eyes. "Yeah right." He reluctantly untied his apron.

"Wait." Aisha reached up and brushed his face. "Cornmeal."

His warm brown eyes met hers. He squeezed her firmly and kissed her again. "You are amazing," he whispered.

"I know." For a brief moment, she closed her eyes and relished being close to him. "But I'm just trying to keep up with you." Greg smiled, took her hand and led her out of the kitchen into the crowded dining room.

Thanks for reading *Advertising for Love*.
Would you like to stay updated on the newest book releases?
Sign up for my newsletter on my website:
www.elisabethroseland.com[1]
Or scan the QR code:

LET'S CONNECT ON TWITTER: @E_Roseland[2]
Find me on Facebook: www.facebook.com/EbonyNights[3]

. . . .

I APPRECIATE ALL HONEST reviews, so please leave one somewhere. Anywhere! Thanks!

. . . .

ADVERTISING FOR LOVE is book one in the Ebony Night Series. Please go to the next page to read an excerpt from book two—*In Production*.

---

1. http://elisabethroseland.com/

2. https://twitter.com/E_Roseland

3.   https://www.facebook.com/EbonyNights

Please enjoy this excerpt from *In Production*, book two in the Ebony Nights Series:

Chapter One

"Stop. Stop! Stop!"

He raised his head to look at her.

"Have you ever eaten pussy before?"

"Yes, ma'am."

"Don't call me ma'am. I'm not your mama."

"Sorry," he mumbled.

"How much pussy have you eaten in your life?"

"Um..."

"Don't lie."

"Some."

Marie lowered her head back on the pillow. "Okay, keep going." His tongue haphazardly jumped from one spot to the next, not once touching her clit or even meandering anywhere in the vicinity. "Stop. Stop! Dammit."

He lifted his head.

"What's your name again?"

"Rasheed."

"Rasheed, put your clothes on and get out."

"What?"

"I said, grab your stuff and get out." Rasheed slowly climbed out of bed and gathered his discarded clothes from the floor. "And when you get back, tell Haven not to send you to me again. Actually, you know what?" She leaned over and grabbed her cell phone off her nightstand. "I'll do it myself."

She scrolled through her address book to the number. Rasheed, now fully dressed, stood silently in the middle of the bedroom. She looked up at him. "What are you waiting for? We're done here."

He shifted uncomfortably from one foot to the other. "I...um...can you...um... I mean, I need to get—"

Marie raised one eyebrow. "You want to get paid for that half-assed attempt?" Rasheed continued to stand there, looking dejectedly at the floor. She got up and picked her purse off the dresser. "Here." She thumbed through her wallet, pulled out some bills and gave the money to him. "Now get out."

He mumbled his thanks and scurried out of the room. The front door slammed behind him. She sat on the bed and picked up the phone.

It rang once. "Haven? What kind of nonsense did you send me?"

"What was wrong with Rasheed?"

"What was wrong with him? He couldn't eat pussy for shit. He had absolutely no idea what he was doing. Did you even test him before you sent him out?"

"Of course. I didn't try him myself, but Alicia did. She said he was great."

"Alicia? That girl is like seventeen. What does she know?"

Haven sighed. "She's twenty-five."

"Whatever. Same difference. Just don't ever send him to me again."

"I'm sorry he didn't work out. I thought he'd be perfect for you. He fits your specifications—over six feet, athletic build, brown skin, young—"

"And he has to know how to fuck. You forgot that part."

"Okay, so Rasheed is off the list for you. No problem." She paused. "You know, I really wish you'd let me send over someone in his thirties. I know someone who would be great."

"Hell no." Marie propped her pillows against the headboard and lay back. "If I wanted to fuck a guy my age, I'd pick him up in the bar at the Ritz. Then I could fuck him for free, instead of paying you a fortune for a special delivery."

"Marie, you know my prices are not exorbitant."

"Still, it's the general principle of the thing."

"Okay, I'll tell you what. Since you are one of my best customers, I'll set you up on a date with Brian. No charge."

"He fits my requirements?"

"Yes. Only, he can't come over tonight. He's with another client. How's Wednesday?"

"No good. I'm in LA all week. Is he available on Saturday?"

"Hold on, let me check." Marie heard typing. "Yes, I've put you in his schedule. Should he meet you at the same spot?"

"Yes, that's fine."

"Great. And please let me know how he works out."

"You know I will." Marie hung up the phone and sighed.

Chapter Two

Coffee.

That was the first thing on Marie's mind when she opened her eyes on Saturday morning. Her week-long LA trip had been exhausting but a huge success. She made a lot of great connections at the Producers Guild of America conference and strengthened her ties to the Hollywood community. Chicago television news was great, even exciting most days, but Hollywood was a whole other level—the next level to her career—and she could feel herself on her way.

"Morning, Marie. The usual?" Jimmy reached behind him for the large cup.

"Thanks, Jimmy." She picked up a copy of the newspaper sitting on the rack in front of her. "And I'll take the paper too."

"Sure thing." Jimmy keyed the total into the register, and she pulled her wallet out of her purse.

"Let me get this." A twenty-dollar bill appeared in front of her, and she turned to see the one person she always tried to avoid.

"What are you doing here?"

"Getting coffee." Vince's smile lit up his face. "Good morning."

"Morning," she grumbled, snatching the money out of his hand and handing it back to him. "I'm not letting you pay for my coffee."

"Yes, you are." He gave the bill to Jimmy with a sharp nod. "Despite my best efforts, I never got a chance to take you out to dinner in LA, so the least I can do is buy your morning caffeine fix." He turned back to Jimmy. "And give me a large as well."

Jimmy made change and handed their coffee to them. "Thank you," she said as she picked up her cup and newspaper and headed for the cream and sugar table. "Vince, there are approximately one thousand coffee shops in the city of Chicago. How is it you happened to be here at this one on a Saturday at the exact same time I'm here?" She added a splash of cream and two sugar packets to her cup.

"Just lucky, I guess. I'm going to take it as a sign I made the right decision to go into work today. Come sit with me for a few minutes."

"I can't, I've got a lot of work to d—"

"So do I. Just a couple of minutes." He gestured to an empty table, his blue eyes scanning her face expectantly.

"Okay, fine. Just a couple of minutes," Marie muttered as she sat.

"Great." Vince slid into the chair across from her. He was dressed casually in jeans and a white T-shirt, his wavy salt-and-pepper hair still slightly damp from a morning shower. "So, I see I'm not the only one who goes into work on a Saturday."

"I'm not going in today. I live around here."

"Oh, really? Living and working all within a few blocks of each other?"

Marie took a sip of her coffee. "Absolutely. It cuts down on the commute. I can be at work in less than ten minutes."

Vince chuckled. The deep sound radiated from his chest. "Always on the job."

"Of course. You of all people should know TV news is a twenty-four seven gig. Why else would you be going into the studio on a Saturday?"

"Fair point. And clearly, I need to stay on my game if my five o'clock broadcast is going to continue to beat yours in the ratings."

"Your station beat mine only three days out of the five, and the only reason it did was because my assistant producer, Theresa, was running the show instead of me. Now that I'm home—" she took a sip from her cup, "—we'll be back on top."

Vince grinned broadly, and the lines at the corners of his eyes wrinkled. "You know, that's what I like about you. You're the only other TV producer in Chicago who works as hard as I do." He paused. "So why did I get the feeling out in LA that you were avoiding me?"

"I wasn't." Marie played with her cup, picking slightly at the paper holder. "I was busy. There were some people I needed to hook up with while I was out there, and I run into you all the time here so..." She took a drink to finish her sentence.

"Like right now."

"Exactly. Like right now."

He stared at her for a moment, his chiseled face softening. "Okay, then. So now that we're both back, let me take you out to lunch one day."

"No."

Vince blinked. "Why not?"

"B-because..." Marie searched for a good reason, "...because I'm busy."

Vince raised his eyebrows. "Too busy to eat?"

"Yes. Too busy to eat."

Vince sat back in his chair and folded his arms. "You know that's a terrible excuse."

"It's not an excuse."

A small smirk appeared at the corner of his mouth. "Of course it is. And you're going to have to do better than that."

"I...uh—"

"Okay, let me help you out. How about...I don't eat lunch because that's how I keep my figure, or I don't actually eat any food at all because I'm allergic to everything and subsist on a diet of coffee and Tic Tacs? Or how about, I do eat lunch, but I would never eat it with you because being seen in public with you is a complete embarrassment and would cause me to lose all my friends and some of my family members?"

Marie laughed in spite of herself. "No. None of those things. Besides, I'm sitting here with you right now, aren't I?"

"Yes, you are. And lunch is the next step. So how about it?"

Vince's powerful forearms and large hands rested on the table, his biceps flexing in response to his movements. She brought her gaze back up to meet his. "I'm sorry, Vince. I can't. I gotta go." Marie stood. "Thanks for the coffee. I'll see you around sometime."

Vince stood as well, but before he had an opportunity to say anything else, she headed for the door and forced herself to keep from looking back.

Look for these titles by Elisabeth Roseland
Now Available:
Ebony Nights Series (Erotic Romance):
Advertising for Love
In Production
Corporate Merger
Bittersweet
Time Bandit Series
The Deviant Underground

. . . .

Coming Soon:
Time Bandit Series
A Deviant Time

About the Author

ELISABETH ROSELAND spends her days dreaming up ways to throw sexy heroes and strong heroines together. Her characters explore the wonderful, agonizing, joyful, heartbreaking and complicated human experiences that are sex and love, with a little fantasy thrown in for good measure. She also hopes to inspire readers to grab the nearest consenting adult and do something fun. She lives in Chicago with her very own Happily Ever After.

Check out her website: www.elisabethroseland.com[1]

Connect on Twitter: @E_Roseland[2]

Find her on Facebook: www.facebook.com/EbonyNights[3]

---

1. http://elisabethroseland.com/

2. https://twitter.com/E_Roseland

3. https://www.facebook.com/EbonyNights

About the Author

Elisabeth Roseland spends her days dreaming up ways to throw sexy heroes and strong heroines together. Her characters explore the wonderful, agonizing, joyful, heartbreaking and complicated human experiences that are sex and love, with a little fantasy thrown in for good measure. She also hopes to inspire readers to grab the nearest consenting adult and do something fun. She lives in Chicago with her very own Happily Ever After.

Read more at www.elisabethroseland.com.